The Short Stories Of Arnold Bennett

The short story is often viewed as an inferior relation to the Novel. But it is a different form, its essence into fewer pages while keeping character and plot rounded and driven is not an easy task. Many try and many fail.

In this series we look at short stories from many of our most accomplished writers. Miniature masterpieces with a lot to say. In this volume we examine some of the short stories of Arnold Bennett

Arnold Bennett was born in 1867 in Hanley, one of the six towns that formed the Potteries that later joined together to become Stoke-on-Trent - the area in which most of his works are located. For a short time he worked for his solicitor father before realising that to advance his life he would need to become his own man. Moving to London at 21, he obtained work as a solicitor's clerk and gradually moved into a career of Journalism.

At the turn of the century he turned full time to writing and shortly thereafter, in 1903, he moved to Paris. In 1908 Bennett published *The Old Wives' Tale*, to great acclaim. With this, his reputation was set.

Clayhanger and *The Old Wives' Tale* are perhaps his greatest and most lauded novels. But standing next to these are many fine short stories and it is to these that we turn our attention in this audiobook. Bennett bathes us in vignettes of life, replete with characters that are easy to immerse ourselves in, whatever their ambitions may be.

All of these stories are also available as an audiobook from our sister company Word Of Mouth. Many samples are at our youtube channel
http://www.youtube.com/user/PortablePoetry?feature=mhee   The full volume can be purchased from iTunes, Amazon and other digital stores. They are read for you by Richard Mitchley

Index Of Stories
The Supreme Illusion
A Letter Home
Mimi
Phantom
The Matador Of The Five Towns
The Letter And The Lie
A Feud

The Supreme Illusion By Arnold Bennett

I
Perhaps it was because I was in a state of excited annoyance that I did not recognize him until he came right across the large hall of the hotel and put his hand on my shoulder.

I had arrived in Paris that afternoon, and driven to that nice, reasonable little hotel which we all know, and whose name we all give in confidence to all our friends; and there was no room in that hotel. Nor in seven other haughtily-managed hotels that I visited! A kind of archduke, who guarded the last of the seven against possible customers, deigned to inform me that the season was at its fullest, half London being as usual in Paris, and that the only central hotels where I had a chance of reception were those monstrosities the Grand and the Hotel Terminus at the Gare St Lazare. I chose the latter, and was accorded room 973 in the roof.

I thought my exasperations were over. But no! A magnificent porter within the gate had just consented to get my luggage off the cab, and was in the act of beginning to do so, when a savagely-dressed, ugly and ageing woman, followed by a maid, rushed neurotically down the steps and called him away to hold a parcel. He obeyed! At the same instant the barbaric and repulsive creature's automobile, about as large as a railway carriage, drove up and forced my frail cab down the street. I had to wait, humiliated and helpless, the taximeter of my cab industriously adding penny to penny, while that offensive hag installed herself, with the help of the maid, the porter and two page-boys, in her enormous vehicle. I should not have minded had she been young and pretty. If she had been young and pretty she would have had the right to be rude and domineering. But she was neither young nor pretty. Conceivably she had once been young; pretty she could never have been. And her eyes were hard - hard.

Hence my state of excited annoyance.

"Hullo! How goes it?" The perfect colloquial English was gently murmured at me with a French accent as the gentle hand patted my shoulder.

"Why," I said, cast violently out of a disagreeable excitement into an agreeable one, "I do believe you are Boissy Minor!"

I had not seen him for nearly twenty years, but I recognized in that soft and melancholy Jewish face, with the soft moustache and the soft beard, the wistful features of the boy of fifteen who had been my companion at an "international" school (a clever invention for inflicting exile upon patriots) with branches at Hastings, Dresden and Versailles.

Soon I was telling him, not without satisfaction, that, being a dramatic critic, and attached to a London daily paper which had decided to flatter its readers by giving special criticisms of the more important new French plays, I had come to Paris for the production of _Notre Dame de la Lune_ at the Vaudeville.

And as I told him the idea occurred to me for positively the first time:

"By the way, I suppose you aren't any relation of Octave Boissy?"

I rather hoped he was; for after all, say what you like, there is a certain pleasure in feeling that you have been to school with even a relative of so tremendous a European celebrity as Octave Boissy - the man who made a million and a half francs with his second play, which was nevertheless quite a good play. All the walls of Paris were shouting his name.

"I'm the johnny himself," he replied with timidity, naively proud of his Saxon slang.

I did not give an astounded No! An astounded No! would have been rude. Still, my fear is that I failed to conceal entirely my amazement. I had to fight desperately against the natural human tendency to assume that no boy with whom one has been to school can have developed into a great man.

"Really!" I remarked, as calmly as I could, and added a shocking lie: "Well, I'm not surprised!" And at the same time I could hear myself saying a few days later at the office of my paper: "I met Octave Boissy in Paris. Went to school with him, you know."

"You'd forgotten my Christian name, probably," he said.

"No, I hadn't," I answered. "Your Christian name was Minor. You never had any other!" He smiled kindly. "But what on earth are you doing here?"

Octave Boissy was a very wealthy man. He even looked a very wealthy man. He was one of the darlings of success and of an absurdly luxurious civilization. And he seemed singularly out of place in the vast, banal foyer of the Hotel Terminus, among the shifting, bustling crowd of utterly ordinary, bourgeois, moderately well-off tourists and travellers and needy touts. He ought at least to have been in a very select private room at the Meurice or the Bristol, if in any hotel at all!

"The fact is, I'm neurasthenic," he said simply, just as if he had been saying, "The fact is, I've got a wooden leg."

"Oh!" I laughed, determined to treat him as Boissy Minor, and not as Octave Boissy.

"I have a morbid horror of walking in the open air. And yet I cannot bear being in a small enclosed space, especially when it's moving. This is extremely inconvenient. Mais que veux-tu?.....Suis comme ca!"

"Je te plains" I put in, so as to return his familiar and flattering "thou" immediately.

"I was strongly advised to go and stay in the country," he went on, with the same serious, wistful simplicity, "and so I ordered a special saloon carriage on the railway, so as to have as much breathing room as possible; and I ventured from my house to this station in an auto. I thought I could surely manage that. But I couldn't! I had a terrible crisis on arriving at the station, and I had to sit on a luggage-truck for four hours. I couldn't have persuaded myself to get into the saloon carriage for a fortune! I couldn't go back home in the auto! I couldn't walk! So I stepped into the hotel. I've been here ever since."

"But when was this?"

"Three months ago. My doctors say that in another six weeks I shall be sufficiently recovered to leave. It is a most distressing malady. Mais que veux-tu? I have a suite in the hotel and my own servants. I walk out here into the hall because it's so large.
The hotel people do the best they can, but of course" He threw up his hands. His resigned, gentle smile was at once comic and tragic to me.

"But do you mean to say you couldn't walk out of that door and go home?" I questioned.

"Daren't!" he said, with finality. "Come to my rooms, will you, and have some tea."

II
A little later his own valet served us with tea in a large private drawing-room on the sixth or seventh floor, to reach which we had climbed a thousand and one stairs; it was impossible for Octave Boissy to use the lift, as he was convinced that he would die in it if he took such a liberty with himself. The

room was hung with modern pictures, such as had certainly never been seen in any hotel before. Many knick-knacks and embroideries were also obviously foreign to the hotel.

"But how have you managed to attend the rehearsals of the new play?" I demanded.

"Oh!" said he, languidly, "I never attend any rehearsals of my plays. Mademoiselle Lemonnier sees to all that."

"She takes the leading part in this play, doesn't she, according to the posters?"

"She takes the leading part in all my plays," said he.

"A first-class artiste, no doubt? I've never seen her act."

"Neither have I!" said Octave Boissy. And as I now yielded frankly to my astonishment, he added: "You see, I am not interested in the theatre. Not only have I never attended a rehearsal, but I have never seen a performance of any of my plays. Don't you remember that it was engineering, above all else, that attracted me? I have a truly wonderful engineering shop in the basement of my house in the Avenue du Bois. I should very much have liked you to see it; but you comprehend, don't you, that I'm just as much cut off from the Avenue du Bois as I am from Timbuctoo. My malady is the most exasperating of all maladies."

"Well, Boissy Minor," I observed, "I suppose it has occurred to you that your case is calculated to excite wonder in the simple breast of a brutal Englishman."

He laughed, and I was glad that I had had the courage to reduce him definitely to the rank of Boissy Minor.

"And not only in the breast of an Englishman!" he said. "Mais que veux-tu? One must live."

"But I should have thought you could have made a comfortable living out of engineering. In England consulting engineers are princes."

"Oh yes!"

"And engineering might have cured your neurasthenia, if you had taken it in sufficiently large quantities."

"It would," he agreed quietly.

"Then why the theatre, seeing that the theatre doesn't interest you?"

"In order to live," he replied. "And when I say 'live,' I mean live. It is not a question of money, it is a question of living."

"But as you never go near the theatre"

"I write solely for Blanche Lemonnier," he said. I was at a loss. Perceiving this, he continued intimately: "Surely you know of my admiration for Blanche Lemonnier?"

I shook my head.

"I have never even heard of Blanche Lemonnier, save in connection with your plays," I said.

"She is only known in connection with my plays," he answered. "When I met her, a dozen years ago, she was touring the provinces, playing small parts in third-rate companies. I asked her what was her greatest ambition, and she said that it was to be applauded as a star on the Paris stage. I told her that I would satisfy her ambition, and that when I had done so I hoped she would satisfy mine. That was how I began to write plays. That was my sole reason. It is the sole reason why I keep on writing them. If she had desired to be a figure in Society I should have gone into politics."

"I am getting very anxious to see this lady," I said. "I feel as if I can scarcely wait till to-night."

"She will probably be here in a few minutes," said he.

"But how did you do it?" I asked. "What was your plan of campaign?"

"After the success of my first play I wrote the second specially for her, and I imposed her on the management. I made her a condition. The management kicked, but I was in a position to insist. I insisted."

"It sounds simple." I laughed uneasily.

"If you are a dramatic critic," he said, "you will guess that it was not at first quite so simple as it sounds. Of course it is simple enough now. Blanche Lemonnier is now completely identified with my plays. She is as well known as nearly any actress in Paris. She has the glory she desired." He smiled curiously. "Her ambition is satisfied - so is mine." He stopped.

"Well," I said, "I've never been so interested in any play before. And I shall expect Mademoiselle Lemonnier to be magnificent."

"Don't expect too much," he returned calmly. "Blanche's acting is not admired by everybody. And I cannot answer for her powers, as I've never seen her at work."

"It's that that's so extraordinary!"

"Not a bit! I could not bear to see her on the stage. I hate the idea of her acting in public. But it is her wish. And after all, it is not the actress that concerns me. It is the woman. It is the woman alone who makes my life worth living. So long as she exists and is kind to me my neurasthenia is a matter of indifference, and I do not even trouble about engineering."

He tried to laugh away the seriousness of his tone, but he did not quite succeed. Hitherto I had been amused at his singular plight and his fatalistic acceptance of it. But now I was touched.

"I'm talking very freely to you," he said.

"My dear fellow," I burst out, "do let me see her portrait."

He shook his head.

"Unfortunately her portrait is all over Paris. She likes it so. But I prefer to have no portrait myself. My feeling is"

At that moment the valet opened the door and we heard vivacious voices in the corridor.

"She is here," said Octave Boissy, in a whisper suddenly dramatic. He stood up; I also. His expression had profoundly changed. He controlled his gestures and his attitude, but he could not control his eye. And when I saw that glance I understood what he meant by "living." I understood that, for him, neither fame nor artistic achievement nor wealth had any value in his life. His life consisted in one thing only.

"Eh bien, Blanche!" he murmured amorously.

Blanche Lemonnier invaded the room with arrogance. She was the odious creature whose departure in her automobile had so upset my arrival.

A Letter Home By Arnold Bennett

I

Rain was falling, it had fallen steadily through the night but the sky showed promise of fairer weather. As the first streaks of dawn appeared, the wind died away, and the young leaves on the trees were almost silent. The birds were insistently clamorous, vociferating times without number that it was a healthy spring morning and good to be alive.

A little, bedraggled crowd stood before the park gates, awaiting the hour named on the notice board when they would be admitted to such lodging and shelter as iron seats and overspreading branches might afford. A weary, patient-eyed, dogged crowd--a dozen men, a boy of thirteen, and a couple of women, both past middle age which had been gathering slowly since five o'clock. The boy appeared to be the least uncomfortable. His feet were bare, but he had slept well in an area in Grosvenor Place, and was not very damp yet. The women had nodded on many doorsteps, and were soaked. They stood apart from the men, who seemed unconscious of their existence. The men were exactly such as one would have expected to find there, beery and restless as to the eyes, quaintly shod, and with nondescript greenish clothes which for the most part bore traces of the yoke of the sandwich board. Only one amongst them was different.

He was young, and his cap, and manner of wearing it, gave sign of the sea. His face showed the rough outlines of his history. Yet it was a transparently honest face, very pale, but still boyish and fresh enough to make one wonder by what rapid descent he had reached his present level. Perhaps the receding chin, the heavy, pouting lower lip, and the ceaselessly twitching mouth offered a key to the problem.
'Say, Darkey!' he said.

'Well?'

'How much longer?'

'Can't ye see the clock? It's staring ye in the face.'

'No. Something queer's come over my eyes.'

Darkey was a short, sturdy man, who kept his head down and his hands deep in his pockets. The raindrops clinging to the rim of an ancient hat fell every now and then into his gray beard, which presented a drowned appearance. He was a person of long and varied experiences; he knew that queer feeling in the eyes, and his heart softened.

'Come, lean against the pillar,' he said, 'if you don't want to tumble. Three of brandy's what you want. There's four minutes to wait yet.'

With body flattened to the masonry, legs apart, and head thrown back, Darkey's companion felt more secure, and his mercurial spirits began to revive. He took off his cap, and brushing back his light brown curly hair with the hand which held it, he looked down at Darkey through half-closed eyes, the play of his features divided between a smile and a yawn.

He had a lively sense of humour, and the irony of his situation was not lost on him. He took a grim, ferocious delight in calling up the might-have-beens and the 'fatuous ineffectual yesterdays' of life. There is a certain sardonic satisfaction to be gleaned from a frank recognition of the fact that you are the architect of your own misfortune. He felt that satisfaction, and laughed at Darkey, who was one of those who moan about 'ill-luck' and 'victims of circumstance.'

'No doubt,' he would say, 'you're a very deserving fellow, Darkey, who's been treated badly. I'm not.'

To have attained such wisdom at twenty-five is not to have lived altogether in vain.

A park-keeper presently arrived to unlock the gates, and the band of outcasts straggled indolently towards the nearest sheltered seats. Some went to sleep at once, in a sitting posture. Darkey produced a clay pipe, and, charging it with a few shreds of tobacco laboriously gathered from his waistcoat pocket, began to smoke. He was accustomed to this sort of thing, and with a pipe in his mouth could contrive to be moderately philosophical upon occasion. He looked curiously at his companion, who lay stretched at full length on another bench.

'I say, pal,' he remarked, 'I've known ye two days; ye've never told me yer name, and I don't ask ye to. But I see ye've not slep' in a park before.'

'You hit it, Darkey; but how?'

'Well, if the keeper catches ye lying down, he'll be on to ye. Lying down's not allowed.'

The man raised himself on his elbow.

'Really now,' he said; 'that's interesting. But I think I'll give the keeper the opportunity of moving me. Why, it's quite fine, the sun's coming out, and the sparrows are hopping round cheeky little devils! I'm not sure that I don't feel jolly.'

'I wish I'd got the price of a pint about me,' sighed Darkey, and the other man dropped his head and appeared to sleep. Then Darkey dozed a little, and heard in his waking sleep the heavy, crunching tread of an approaching park-keeper; he started up to warn his companion, but thought better of it, and closed his eyes again.

'Now then, there,' the park-keeper shouted to the man with the sailor's cap, 'get up! This ain't a fourpenny doss, you know. No lying down.'

A rough shake accompanied the words, and the man sat up.

'All right, my friend.'

The keeper, who was a good-humoured man, passed on without further objurgation.

The face of the younger man had grown whiter.

'Look here, Darkey,' he said, 'I believe I'm done for.'

'Never say die.'

'No, just die without speaking.'

His head fell forward and his eyes closed.

'At any rate, this is better than some deaths I've seen,' he began again with a strange accession of liveliness. 'Darkey, did I tell you the story of the five Japanese girls?'

'What, in Suez Bay?' said Darkey, who had heard many sea-stories during the last two days, and recollected them but hazily.

'No, man. This was at Nagasaki. We were taking in a cargo of coal for Hong Kong. Hundreds of little Jap girls pass the coal from hand to hand over the ship's side in tiny baskets that hold about a plateful. In that way you can get three thousand tons aboard in two days.'

'Talking of platefuls reminds me of sausage and mash,' said Darkey.

'Don't interrupt. Well, five of these gay little dolls wanted to go to Hong Kong, and they arranged with the Chinese sailors to stow away; I believe their friends paid those cold-blooded fiends something to pass them down food on the voyage, and give them an airing at nights. We had a particularly lively trip, battened everything down tight, and scarcely uncovered till we got into port. Then I and another man found those five girls among the coal.'

'Dead, eh?'

'They'd simply torn themselves to pieces. Their bits of frock things were in strips, and they were scratched deep from top to toe.
The Chinese had never troubled their heads about them at all, although they must have known it meant death. You may bet there was a row. The Japanese authorities make you search ship before sailing, now.'

'Well?'

'Well, I shan't die like that. That's all.'

He stretched himself out once more, and for ten minutes neither spoke. The park-keeper strolled up again.

'Get up, there!' he said shortly and gruffly.

'Up ye get, mate,' added Darkey, but the man on the bench did not stir. One look at his face sufficed to startle the keeper, and presently two policemen were wheeling an ambulance cart to the hospital. Darkey followed, gave such information as he could, and then went his own ways.

II

In the afternoon the patient regained full consciousness. His eyes wandered vacantly about the illimitable ward, with its rows of beds stretching away on either side of him. A woman with a white cap, a white apron, and white wristbands bent over him, and he felt something gratefully warm passing down his throat. For just one second he was happy. Then his memory returned, and the nurse saw that he was crying. When he caught the nurse's eye he ceased, and looked steadily at the distant ceiling.

'You're better?'

'Yes.'

He tried to speak boldly, decisively, nonchalantly. He was filled with a sense of physical shame, the shame which bodily helplessness always experiences in the presence of arrogant, patronizing health. He would have got up and walked briskly away if he could. He hated to be waited on, to be humoured, to be examined and theorized about. This woman would be wanting to feel his pulse. She should not; he would turn cantankerous. No doubt they had been saying to each other, 'And so young, too! How sad!' Confound them!

'Have you any friends that you would like to send for?'

'No, none.'

The girl, she was only a girl, looked at him, and there was that in her eye which overcame him.

'None at all?'

'Not that I want to see.'

'Are your parents alive?'

'My mother is, but she lives away in the Five Towns.'

'You've not seen her lately, perhaps?'

He did not reply, and the nurse spoke again, but her voice sounded indistinct and far off.

When he awoke it was night. At the other end of the ward was a long table covered with a white cloth, and on this table a lamp.

In the ring of light under the lamp was an open book, an inkstand and a pen. A nurse, not his nurse, was standing by the table, her fingers idly drumming the cloth, and near her a man in evening dress. Perhaps a doctor. They were conversing in low tones. In the middle of the ward was an open stove, and the restless flames were reflected in all the brass knobs of the bedsteads and in some shining metal balls which hung from an unlighted chandelier. His part of the ward was almost in darkness. A confused, subdued murmur of little coughs, breathings, rustlings, was continually audible, and sometimes it rose above the conversation at the table. He noticed all these things. He became conscious, too, of a strangely familiar smell. What was it? Ah, yes! Acetic acid; his mother used it for her rheumatics.

Suddenly, magically, a great longing came over him. He must see his mother, or his brothers, or his little sister; someone who knew him, someone who belonged to him. He could have cried out in his desire. This one thought consumed all his faculties. If his mother could but walk in just now through that doorway! If only old Spot even could amble up to him, tongue out and tail furiously wagging! He tried to sit up, and he could not move! Then despair settled on him, and weighed him down. He closed his eyes.

The doctor and the nurse came slowly up the ward, pausing here and there. They stopped before his bed, and he held his breath.

'Not roused up again, I suppose?'

'No.'

'H'm! He may flicker on for forty-eight hours. Not more.'

They went on, and with a sigh of relief he opened his eyes again. The doctor shook hands with the nurse, who returned to the table and sat down.

Death! The end of all this! Yes, it was coming. He felt it. His had been one of those wasted lives of which he used to read in books. How strange! Almost amusing! He was one of those sons who bring sorrow and shame into a family. Again, how strange! What a coincidence that he, just he and not the man in the next bed - should be one of those rare, legendary good-for-nothings who go recklessly to ruin. And yet, he was sure that he was not such a bad fellow after all. Only somehow he had been careless. Yes, careless; that was the word ... nothing worse.... As to death, he was indifferent. Remembering his father's death, he reflected that it was probably less disturbing to die one's self than to watch another pass.

He smelt the acetic acid once more, and his thoughts reverted to his mother. Poor mother! No, great mother! The grandeur of her life's struggle filled him with a sense of awe. Strange that until that moment he had never seen the heroic side of her humdrum, commonplace existence! He must write to her, now, at once, before it was too late. His letter would trouble her, add another wrinkle to her face, but he must write; she must know that he had been thinking of her.

'Nurse!' he cried out, in a thin, weak voice.

'Ssh!'

She was by his side directly, but not before he had lost consciousness again.

The following morning he managed with infinite labour to scrawl a few lines:

'DEAR MAMMA,

'You will be surprised but not glad to get this letter. I'm done for, and you will never see me again. I'm sorry for what I've done, and how I've treated you, but it's no use saying anything now. If Pater had only lived he might have kept me in order. But you were too kind, you know. You've had a hard struggle these last six years, and I hope Arthur and Dick will stand by you better than I did, now they are growing up. Give them my love, and kiss little Fannie for me.

'WILLIE.

'Mrs. Hancock'

He got no further with the address.

III

By some turn of the wheel, Darkey gathered several shillings during the next day or two, and, feeling both elated and benevolent, he called one afternoon at the hospital, 'just to inquire like.' They told him the man was dead.

'By the way, he left a letter without an address. Mrs. Hancock; here it is.'

'That'll be his mother; he did tell me about her, lived at Knype, Staffordshire, he said. I'll see to it.'

They gave Darkey the letter.

'So his name's Hancock,' he soliloquized, when he got into the street. 'I knew a girl of that name once. I'll go and have a pint of four-half.'

At nine o'clock that night Darkey was still consuming four-half, and relating certain adventures by sea which, he averred, had happened to himself. He was very drunk.

'Yes,' he said, 'and them five lil' gals was lying there without a stitch on 'em, dead as meat's 'true as I'm 'ere. I've seen a thing or two in my time, I can tell ye.'

'Talking about these Anarchists' said a man who appeared anxious to change the subject.

'An-kists,' Darkey interrupted. 'I tell ye what I'd do with that muck.'

He stopped to light his pipe, looked in vain for a match, felt in his pockets, and pulled out a piece of paper; the letter.

'I tell you what I'd do. I'd-'

He slowly and meditatively tore the letter in two, dropped one piece on the floor, thrust the other into a convenient gas-jet, and applied it to the tobacco.

'I'd get 'em 'gether in a heap, and I'd- Damn this pipe!'

He picked up the other half of the letter, and relighted the pipe.

'After you, mate,' said a man sitting near, who was just biting the end from a cigar.

Mimi By Arnold Bennett

I

On a Saturday afternoon in late October Edward Coe, a satisfactory average successful man of thirty-five, was walking slowly along the King's Road, Brighton. A native and inhabitant of the Five Towns in the Midlands, he had the brusque and energetic mien of the Midlands. It could be seen that he was a stranger to the south; and, in fact, he was now viewing for the first time the vast and glittering spectacle of the southern pleasure city in the unique glory of her autumn season. A spectacle to enliven any man by its mere splendour! And yet Edward Coe was gloomy. One reason for his gloom was that he had just left a bicycle, with a deflated back tyre, to be repaired at a shop in Preston Street. Not perhaps an adequate reason for gloom!... Well, that depends. He had been informed by the blue-clad repairer, after due inspection, that the trouble was not a common puncture, but a malady of the valve mysterious.

And the deflation was not the sole cause of his gloom. There was another. He was on his honeymoon. Understand me, not a honeymoon of romance, but a real honeymoon. Who that has ever been on a real honeymoon can look back upon the adventure and faithfully say that it was an unmixed ecstasy of joy? A honeymoon is in its nature and consequences so solemn, so dangerous, and so pitted with startling surprises, that the most irresponsible bridegroom, the most light-hearted, the least in love, must have moments of grave anxiety. And Edward Coe was far from irresponsible. Nor was he only a little in love. Moreover, the circumstances of his marriage were peculiar, and he had married a dark, brooding, passionate girl.

Mrs Coe was the younger of two sisters named Olive Wardle, well known in the most desirable circles in the Five Towns. I mean those circles where intellectual and artistic tastes are united with sound incomes and excellent food delicately served. It will certainly be asked why two sisters should be named Olive. The answer is that though Olive One and Olive Two were treated as sisters, and even treated themselves as sisters, they were not sisters. They were not even half-sisters. They had first met at the age of nine. The father of Olive One, a widower, had married the mother of Olive Two, a widow. Olive One was the elder by a few months. Olive Two gradually allowed herself to be called Wardle because it saved trouble. They got on with one another very well indeed, especially after the death of both parents, when they became joint mistresses, each with a separate income, of a nice house at Sneyd, the fashionable residential village on the rim of the Five Towns. Like all persons who live long together, they grew in many respects alike. Both were dark, brooding and passionate, and to this deep similarity a superficial similarity of habits and demeanour was added. Only, whereas Olive One was rather more inclined to be the woman of the world, Olive Two was rather more inclined to study and was particularly interested in the theory of music.

They were sought after, naturally. And yet they had reached the age of twenty-five before the world perceived that either of them was not sought after in vain.

The fact, obvious enough, that Pierre Emile Vaillac had become an object of profound human interest to Olive One, this fact excited the world, and the world would have been still more excited had it been aware of another fact that was not at all obvious: namely, that Pierre Emile Vaillac was the cause of a secret and terrible breach between the two sisters. Vaillac, a widower with two young children, Mimi and Jean, was a Frenchman, and a great authority on the decoration of egg-shell china, who had settled in the Five Towns as expert partner in one of the classic china firms at Longshaw. He was undoubtedly a very attractive man.

Olive One, when the relations between herself and Vaillac were developing into something unmistakable, had suddenly, and without warning, accused Olive Two of poaching. It was a frightful accusation, and a frightful scene followed it, one of those scenes that are seldom forgiven and never forgotten. It altered their lives; but as they were women of considerable common sense and of good breeding, each did her best to behave afterwards as though nothing had happened.

Olive Two did not convince Olive One of her innocence, because she did not bring forward the supreme proof of it. She was too proud--in her brooding and her mystery--to do so. The supreme proof was that at this time she herself was secretly engaged to be married to Edward Coe, who had conquered her heart with unimaginable swiftness a few weeks before she was about to sit for a musical examination at Manchester. "Let us say nothing till after my exam," she had suggested to her betrothed. "There will be an enormous fuss, and it will put me off, and I shall fail, and I don't want to fail, and you don't want me to fail." He agreed rapturously. Of course she did fail, nevertheless. But being obstinate she said she would go in again, and they continued to make a secret of the engagement. They found the secret delicious. Then followed the devastating episode of Vaillac. Shortly afterwards Olive One and Vaillac were married, and then Olive Two was alone in the nice house. The examination was forgotten, and she hated the house. She wanted to be married; Coe also. But nothing had been said. Difficult to announce her engagement just then! The world would say that she had married out of imitation, and her sister would think that she had married out of pique. Besides, there would be the fuss, which Olive Two hated. Already the fuss of her sister's marriage, and the effort at the wedding of pretending that nothing had happened between them, had fatigued the nerves of Olive Two.

Then Edward Coe had had the brilliant and seductive idea of marrying in secret. To slip away, and then to return, saying, "We are married. That's all!" Why not? No fuss! No ceremonial! The accomplished fact, which simplifies everything!

It was, therefore, a secret honeymoon that Edward Coe was on; delightful but surreptitious, furtive! His mental condition may be best described by stating that, though he was conscious of rectitude, he somehow could not look a policeman in the face. After all, plain people do not usually run off on secret honeymoons. Had he acted wisely? Perhaps this question, presenting itself now and then, was the chief cause of his improper gloom.

II

However, the spectacle of Brighton on a fine Saturday afternoon in October had its effect on Edward Coe the effect which it has on everybody. Little by little it inspired him with the joy of life, and straightened his back, and put a sparkle into his eyes. And he was filled with the consciousness of the fact that it is a fine thing to be well-dressed and to have loose gold in your pocket, and to eat, drink, and smoke well; and to be among crowds of people who are well-dressed and have loose gold in their pockets, and eat and drink and smoke well; and to know that a magnificent woman will be waiting for you at a certain place at a certain hour, and that upon catching sight of you her dark orbs will take on an enchanting expression reserved for you alone, and that she is utterly yours.
In a word, he looked on the bright side of things again. It could not ultimately matter a bilberry whether his marriage was public or private.

He lit a cigarette gaily. He could not guess that untoward destiny was waiting for him close by the newspaper kiosque.

A little girl was leaning against the palisade there, and gazing somewhat restlessly about her. A quite little girl, aged, perhaps, eleven, dressed in blue serge, with a short frock and long legs, and a sailor hat (H.M.S. Formidable), and long hair down her back, and a mild, twinkling, trustful glance. Somewhat untidy, but nevertheless the image of grace.

She saw him first. Otherwise he might have fled. But he was right upon her before he saw her. Indeed, he heard her before he saw her.

"Good afternoon, Mr Coe."

"Mimi!"

The Vaillacs were in Brighton! He had chosen practically the other end of the world for his honeymoon, and lo! by some awful clumsiness of fate the Vaillacs were at the same end! The very people from whom he wished to conceal his honeymoon until it was over would know all about it at the very start! Relations between the two Olives would be still more strained and difficult! In brief, from optimism he swung violently back to darkest pessimism. What could be worse than to be caught red-handed in a surreptitious honeymoon?

She noticed his confusion, and he knew that she noticed it. She was a little girl. But she was also a little woman, a little Frenchwoman, who spoke English perfectly - and yet with a difference! They had flirted together, she and Mr Coe. She had a new mother now, but for years she had been without a mother, and she would receive callers at her father's house (if he happened to be out) with a delicious imitation of a practised hostess.

He raised his hat and shook hands and tried to play the game.

"What are you doing here, Mimi?" he asked.

"What are you doing here?" she parried, laughing. And then, perceiving his increased trouble, and that she was failing intact, she went on rapidly, with a screwing up of the childish shoulders and something between a laugh and a grin: "It's my back. It seems it's not strong. And so we've taken an ever so jolly little house for the autumn, because of the air, you know. Didn't you know?"

No, he did not know. That was the worst of strained relations. You were not informed of events in advance.

"Where?" he asked.

"Oh!" she said, pointing. "That way. On the road to Rottingdean. Near the big girls' school. We came in on that lovely electric railway along the beach. Have you been on it, Mr Coe?"

Terrible! Rottingdean was precisely the scene of his honeymoon. The hazard of fate was truly appalling. He and his wife might have walked one day straight into the arms of her sister! He went hot and cold.
"And where are the others?" he asked nervously.

"Mamma" she coloured as she used this word, so strange on her lips "mamma's at home. Father may come to-night. And Ada has brought us here so that Jean can have his hair cut. He didn't want to come without me."

"Ada?"

"Ada's a new servant. She's just gone in there again to see how long the barber will be." Mimi indicated a barber's shop opposite. "And I'm waiting here," she added.

"Mimi," he said, in a confidential tone, "can you keep a secret?"

She grew solemn. "Yes." She smiled seriously. "What?"

"About meeting me. Don't tell anybody you've met me to-day. See?"

"Not Jean?"

"No, not Jean. But later on you can tell--when I give you the tip. I don't want anybody to know just now."

It was a shame. He knew it was a shame. He deliberately flattered her by appealing to her as to a grown woman. He deliberately put a cajoling tone into his voice. He would not have done it if Mimi had not been Mimi, if she had been an ordinary sort of English girl. But she was Mimi. And the temptation was very strong. She promised, gravely. He knew that he could rely on her.

Hurrying away lest Jean and the servant might emerge from the barber's, he remembered with compunction that he had omitted to show any curiosity about Mimi's back.

III

The magnificent woman was to be waiting for him in the lounge of the Royal York Hotel at a quarter to four. She was coming in to Brighton by the Rottingdean omnibus, which function, unless the driver changes his mind, occurs once in every two or three hours. He, being under the necessity of telephoning to London on urgent business, had hired a bicycle and ridden in. Despite the accident to this prehistoric machine, he arrived at the Royal York half a minute before the Rottingdean omnibus passed through the Old Steine and set down the magnificent woman his wife. The sight of her stepping off the omnibus really did thrill him. They entered the hotel together, and, accustomed though the Royal York is to the reception of magnificent women, Olive made a sensation therein. As for him, he could not help feeling just as though he had eloped with her. He could not help fancying that all the brilliant company in the lounge was murmuring under the strains of the band: "That johnny there has certainly eloped with that splendid creature!"

"Ed," she asked, fixing her dark eyes upon him, "is anything the matter?"

They were having tea at a little Moorish table in the huge bay window of the lounge.

"No," he said. This was the first lie of his career as a husband.
But truly he could not bring himself to give her the awful shock of telling her that the Vaillacs were close at hand, that their secret was discovered, and that their peace and security depended entirely upon the discretion of little Mimi and upon their not meeting other Vaillacs.

"Then it's having that puncture that has upset you," his wife insisted. You see her feelings towards him were so passionate that she could not leave him alone. She was utterly preoccupied by him.

"No," he said guiltily.

"I'm afraid you don't very much care for this place," she went on, because she knew now that he was not telling her the truth, and that something, indeed, was the matter.

"On the contrary," he replied, "I was informed that the finest tea and the most perfect toast in Brighton were to be had in this lounge, and upon my soul I feel as if I could keep on having tea here forever and ever amen!"

He was trying to be gay, but not very successfully.

"I don't mean just here," she said. "I mean all this south coast."

"Well" he began judicially.

"Oh! Ed!" she implored him. "Do say you don't like it!"

"Why!" he exclaimed. "Don't you?"

She shook her head. "I much prefer the north," she remarked.

"Well," he said, "let's go. Say Scarborough."

"You're joking," she murmured. "You adore this south coast."

"Never!" he asserted positively.

"Well, darling," she said, "if you hadn't said first that you didn't care for it, of course I shouldn't have breathed a word"

"Let's go to-morrow," he suggested.

"Yes." Her eyes shone.

"First train! We should have to leave Rottingdean at six o'clock a.m."

"How lovely!" she exclaimed. She was enchanted by this idea of a capricious change of programme. It gave such a sense of freedom, of irresponsibility, of romance!

"More toast, please," he said to the waiter, joyously.

It cost him no effort to be gay now. He could not have been sad. The world was suddenly transformed into the best of all possible worlds. He was saved! They were saved! Yes, he could trust Mimi. By no chance would they be caught.
They would stick in their rooms all the evening, and on the morrow they would be away long before the Vaillacs were up. Papa and "mamma" Vaillac were terrible for late rising. And when he had got his magnificent Olive safe in Scarborough, or wherever their noses might lead them, then he would tell her of the risk they had run.

They both laughed from mere irrational glee, and Edward Coe nearly forgot to pay the bill. However, he did pay it. They departed from the Royal York. He put his Olive into the returning Rottingdean omnibus, and then hurried to get his repaired bicycle. He had momentarily quaked lest Mimi and company might be in the omnibus. But they were not. They must have left earlier, fortunately, or walked.

IV
When he was still about a mile away from Rottingdean, and the hour was dusk, and he was walking up a hill, he caught sight of a girl leaning on a gate that led by a long path to a house near the cliffs. It was Mimi. She gave a cry of recognition. He did not care now he was at ease now but really, with that house so close to the road and so close to Rottingdean, he and his Olive had practically begun their honeymoon on the summit of a volcano!

Mimi was pensive. He felt remorse at having bound her to secrecy. She was so pensive, and so wistful, and her eyes were so loyal, that he felt he owed her a more complete confidence.

"I'm on my honeymoon, Mimi," he said. It gave him pleasure to tell her.

"Yes," she said simply, "I saw Auntie Olive go by in the omnibus."

That was all she said. He was thunderstruck, as much by her calm simplicity as by anything else. Children were astounding creatures.

"Did Jean see her, or anyone?" he asked.

Mimi shook her head.

Then he told her they were leaving the next morning at six.

"Shall you be in a carriage?" she inquired.

"Yes."

"Oh! Do let me come out and see you go past," she pleaded. "Nobody else in our house will be up till hours afterwards! Do!"

He was about to say "No," for it would mean revealing the whole affair to his wife at once. But after an instant he said "Yes." He would not refuse that exquisite, appealing gesture. Besides, why keep anything whatever from Olive, even for a day?

At dinner he told his wife, and was glad to learn that she also thought highly of Mimi and had confidence in her.

V

Mimi lay in bed in the nursery of the hired house on the way to Rottingdean, which, considering that it was not "home," was a fairly comfortable sort of abode. The nursery was immense, though an attic. The white blinds of the two windows were drawn, and a fire burned in the grate, lighting it pleasantly and behaving in a very friendly manner. At the other end of the room, in the deep shadow, was Jean's bed.

The door opened quietly and someone came into the room and pushed the door to without quite shutting it.

"Is that you, mamma?" Jean demanded in his shrill voice, from the distance of the bed in the corner. His age was exactly eight.

"Yes, dear," said the new stepmother.

The menial Ada had arranged the children for the night, and now the stepmother had come up to kiss them and be kind. She was a conscientious young woman, full of a desire to do right, and she had determined not to be like the traditional stepmother.

17

She kissed Jean, who had taken quite a fancy to her, and tickled him agreeably, and tucked him up anew, and then moved silently across the room to Mimi. Mimi could see her face in the twilight of the fire. A handsome, good-natured face; yet very determined, and perhaps a little too full of common sense. It had a responsible, somewhat grave look. After all, these two young children were a responsibility, especially Mimi with her back; and, moreover, Pierre Emile Vaillac had disappointed both her and her step-children by telegraphing that he could not arrive that night. Olive One, the bride of three months, had put on fine raiment for nothing.

"Well, Mimi," she said in her low, vibrating voice, as she stood over the bed, "I do hope you didn't overtire yourself this afternoon." Then she kissed Mimi.

"Oh no, mamma!" The little girl smiled.

"It seems you waited outside the barber's while Jeannot was having his hair cut."

"Yes, mamma. I didn't like to go in."

"Ada didn't stay with you all the time?"

"No, mamma. First of all she took Jeannot in, and then she came out to me, and then she went in again to see how long he would be."

"I'm sorry she left you alone in the street. She ought not to have done so, and I've told her.... The King's Road, with all kinds of people about!"

Mimi said nothing. The new Madame Vaillac moved a little towards the fire.

"Of course," the latter went on, "I know you're a regular little woman, and perhaps I needn't tell you but you must never speak to anyone in the street."

"No, mamma."

"Particularly in Brighton.... You never do, do you?"

"No, mamma."

"Good-night."

The stepmother left the room. Mimi could feel her heart beating. Then Jean called out:

"Mimi."

She made no reply. The fact was she was too disturbed to be able to reply.

Jean called again and then got out of bed and thudded across the room to her bedside.

"I say, Mimi," he screeched in his insistent treble, "who was it you were talking to?"

Mimi's heart did not beat, it jumped.

"When? Where?"

"This afternoon, when I was having my hair cut."

"How do you know I was talking to anybody?"

"Ada saw you through the window of the barber's."

"When did she tell you?"

"She didn't. I heard her telling mamma."

There was a silence. Then Mimi hid her face, and Jean could hear sobbing.

"You might tell me!" Jean insisted. He was too absorbed by his own curiosity, and too upset by the full realization of the fact that she had kept something from him, to be touched by her tears.

"It's a secret," she muttered into the pillow.

"You might tell me!"

"Go away, Jeannot!" she burst out hysterically.

He gave an angry lunge against the bed.

"I tell you everything; and it's not fair. C'est pas juste!" he said savagely, but there were tears in his voice too. He was a creature at once sensitive and violent, passionately attached to Mimi.

He thudded back to his bed. But even before he had reached his bed Mimi could hear him weeping.

She gradually stilled her own sobs, and after a time Jean's ceased. And then she guessed that Jean had gone to sleep. But Mimi did not go to sleep. She knew that chance, and Mr Coe, and that odious new servant, Ada, had combined to ruin her life. She saw the whole affair clearly.
Ada was officious and fussy, also secretive and given to plotting. Ada's leading idea was that children had to be circumvented. Imagine the detestable woman spying on her from the window, and then saying nothing to her, but sneaking off to tell tales to her mamma! Imagine it! Mimi's strict sense of justice could not blame her mamma. She was sure that the new stepmother meant well by her. Her mamma had given her every opportunity to confess, to admit of her own accord that she had been talking to somebody in the street, and she had not confessed. On the contrary, she had lied. Her mamma would probably say nothing more on the matter, for she had a considerable sense of honour with children, and would not take an unfair advantage. Having tried to obtain a confession from Mimi by pretending that she knew nothing, and having failed, she was not the woman to turn round and say, "Now I know all about it. So just confess at once!" Her mamma would accept the situation, would try to behave as if nothing had happened, and would probably even say nothing to her father.

But Mimi knew that she was ruined forever in her stepmother's esteem.

And she had quarrelled with Jean, which was exceedingly hateful and exceedingly rare. And there was also the private worry of her mysterious back. And there was another thing. The mere fact that her friend, Mr Coe, had gone and married somebody. For long she had had a weakness for Mr Coe.

They had been intimate at times. Once, last year, in the stern of a large sailing-boat at Morecambe, while her friends were laughing and shouting at the prow, she and Mr Coe had had a most beautiful quiet conversation about her thoughts on the world in general; she had stroked his hand.... No! She had no dream whatever of growing up into a woman and then marrying Mr Coe! Certainly not. But still, that he should have gone and married, like that ... it was....

The fire died out into blackness, thus ceasing to be a friend. Still she did not sleep. Was it likely that she should sleep, with the tragedy and woe of the entire universe crushing her?

VI

Mr Edward Coe and Olive Two arose from their bed the next morning in great spirits. Mr Coe had told both his wife and Mimi that the hour of departure from Rottingdean would be six o'clock. But this was an exaggeration. So far as his wife was concerned he had already found it well to exaggerate on such matters. A little judicious exaggeration lessened the risk of missing trains and other phenomena which cannot be missed without confusion and disappointment.

As a fact it was already six o'clock when Edward Coe looked forth from the bedroom window. He was completely dressed. His wife also was completely dressed. He therefore felt quite safe about the train. The window, which was fairly high up in the world, gave on the south-east, so that he had a view, not only of the vast naked downs billowing away towards Newhaven, but also of the Channel, which was calm, and upon which little parcels of fog rested. The sky was clear overhead, of a greenish sapphire colour, and the autumnal air bit and gnawed on the skin like some friendly domestic animal, and invigorated like an expensive tonic. On the dying foliage of a tree near the window millions of precious stones hung. Cocks were boasting. Cows were expressing a justifiable anxiety. And in the distance a small steamer was making a great deal of smoke about nothing, as it puffed out of Newhaven harbour.

"Olive," he said.

"What is it?"

She was putting hats into the top of her trunk. She had a special hat-box, but the hats were too large for it, and she packed minor trifles in the hat-box, such as skirts. This was one of the details which first indicated to an astounded Edward Coe that a woman is never less like a man than when travelling.

"Come here," he commanded her.

She obeyed.

"Look at that," he commanded her, pointing to the scene of which the window was the frame.

She obeyed. She also looked at him with her dark, passionate, and yet half-mocking eyes.

"Yes," she said, "and who's going to make that trunk lock?"

She snapped her fingers at the sweet morning influences of Nature, to which he was peculiarly sensitive. And yet he was delighted. He found it entirely delicious that she should say, when called upon to admire Nature: "Who's going to make that trunk lock?"

He stroked her hair.

"It's no use trying to keep your hair decent at the seaside," she remarked, pouting exquisitely.

He explained that his hand was offering no criticism of her hair. And then there was a knock at the bedroom door, and Olive Two jumped a little away from her husband.

"Come in," he cried, pretending to be as bold as a lion.

However, he had forgotten that the door was locked, and he had to go and open it.

A tray with coffee and milk and sugar and slices of bread-and-butter was in the doorway, and behind the tray the little parlour-maid of the little hotel. He greeted the girl and instructed her to carry the tray to the table by the window.

"You are prompt," said Olive Two, kindly. She had got up so miraculously early herself that she was startled to see any other woman up quite as early. And also she was a little surprised that the parlour-maid showed no surprise at these very unusual hours.

"Yes'm," replied the parlour-maid, wondering why Olive Two was so excited. The parlour-maid arose at five-thirty every morning of her life, except on special occasions, when she arose at four-thirty to assist in pastoral affairs.

"All right, this coffee, eh?" murmured Edward Coe as he put down the steaming cup after his first sip. They were alone again, seated opposite each other at the small table by the window.

Olive Two nodded.

It must not be supposed that this was the one unique dreamed-of hotel in England where the coffee is good of its own accord. No! In the matter of coffee this hotel was just like all other hotels. Only Olive Two had taken special precautions about that coffee. She had been into the hotel kitchen on the previous evening about that coffee.

"By the way," she asked, "where's the sun?"

"The sun doesn't happen to be up yet," said Edward. He looked at his diary and then at his watch. "Unless something goes wrong, you'll be seeing it inside of three minutes."

"Do you mean to say we shall see the sun rise?" she exclaimed.

He nodded.

"Well!" cried she, absurdly gleeful, "I never heard of such a thing!"

She watched the sunrise like a child who sees for the first time the inside of a watch. And when the sun had risen she glanced anxiously round the disordered room.

"For heaven's sake," she muttered, "don't let's forget these tooth-brushes!"

"You are so ridiculous," said he, "that I must kiss you."

The truth is that they were no better than two children out on an adventure.

It was the same when down in the hotel-yard they got into the small and decrepit victoria which was destined to take them and their luggage to Brighton. It was the same, but more so. They were both so pleased with themselves that their joy was bubbling continually out in manifestations that could only be described as infantile. The mere drive through the village, with the pony whisking his tail round corners, and the driver steadying the perilous hat-box with his left hand, was so funny that somehow they could not help laughing.

Then they had left the village and were climbing the exposed highroad, with the wavy blue-green downs on the right, and the immense glittering flat floor of the Channel on the left. And the mere sensation of being alive almost overwhelmed them.

And further on they passed a house that stood by itself away from the road towards the cliffs. It had a sloping garden and a small greenhouse. The gate leading to the road was ajar, but the blinds of all the windows were drawn, and there was no sign of life anywhere.

"That's the house," said Edward Coe, briefly.

"I might have known it," Olive Two replied. "Olive One is certainly the worst getter-up that I ever had anything to do with, and I believe Pierre Emile isn't much better."

"Well," said Edward, "it's no absolute proof of sluggardliness not to be up and about at six forty-five of a morning, you know."

"I was forgetting how early it was!" said Olive Two, and yawned. The yawn escaped her before she was aware of it. She pulled herself together and kissed her hands mockingly, quizzically, to the house. "Good-bye, house! Good-bye, house!"

They were saved now. They could not be caught now on their surreptitious honeymoon. And their spirits went even higher.

"I thought you said Mimi would be waiting for us?" Olive Two remarked.
Edward Coe shrugged his shoulders. "Probably overslept herself! Or she may have got tired of waiting. I told her six o'clock."

On the whole Olive Two was relieved that Mimi was invisible.

"It wouldn't really matter if she did split on us, would it?" said the bride.

"Not a bit," the bridegroom agreed. Now that they had safely left the house behind them, they were both very valiant. It was as if they were both saying: "Who cares?" The bridegroom's mood was entirely different from his sombre apprehensiveness of the previous evening. And the early sunshine on the dew-drops was magnificent.

But a couple of hundred yards further on, at a bend of the road, they saw a little girl shading her eyes with her hand and gazing towards the sun. She wore a short blue serge frock, and she had long restless legs, and the word Formidable was on her forehead, and her eyes were all screwed up in the strong sunshine. And in her hand were flowers.

"There she is, after all!" said Edward, quickly.

Olive Two nodded. Olive Two also blushed, for Mimi was the first person acquainted with her to see her after her marriage. She blushed because she was now a married woman.

Mimi, who with much prudence had managed so that the meeting should not occur exactly in front of the house, came towards the carriage. The pony was walking up a slope. She bounded forward with her childish grace and with the awkwardness of her long legs, and her hair loose in the breeze, and she laughed nervously.

"Good morning, good morning," she cried. "Shall I jump on the step? Then the horse won't have to stop."

And she jumped lightly on to the step and giggled, still nervously, looking first at the bridegroom and then at the bride. The bridegroom held her securely by the shoulder.

"Well, Mimi," said Olive Two, whose shyness vanished in an instant before the shyness of the child. "This is nice of you."

The two women kissed. But Mimi did not offer her cheek to the bridegroom. He and she simply shook hands as well as they could with a due regard for Mimi's firmness on the step.

"And who woke you up, eh?" Edward Coe demanded.

"Nobody," said Mimi; "I got up by myself, and;" turning to Olive Two, "I've made this bouquet for you, auntie. There aren't any flowers in the fields. But I got the chrysanthemum out of the greenhouse, and put some bits of ferns and things round it. You must excuse it being tied up with darning wool."

She offered the bouquet diffidently, and Olive Two accepted it with a warm smile.

"Well," said Mimi, "I don't think I'd better go any further, had I?"

There was another kiss and hand-shaking, and the next moment Mimi was standing in the road and waving a little crumpled handkerchief to the receding victoria, and the bride and bridegroom were cricking their necks to respond. She waved until the carriage was out of sight, and then she stood moveless, a blue and white spot on the green landscape, with the morning sun and the sea behind her.

"Exactly like a little woman, isn't she?" said Edward Coe, enchanted by the vision.

"Exactly!" Olive Two agreed. "Nice little thing! But how tired and unwell she looks! They did well to bring her away."

"Oh!" said Edward Coe, "she probably didn't sleep well because she was afraid of oversleeping herself. She looked perfectly all right yesterday."

Phantom By Arnold Bennett

I
The heart of the Five Towns--that undulating patch of England covered with mean streets, and dominated by tall smoking chimneys, whence are derived your cups and saucers and plates, some of

your coal, and a portion of your iron is Hanbridge, a borough larger and busier than its four sisters, and even more grimy and commonplace than they. And the heart of Hanbridge is probably the offices of the Five Towns Banking Company, where the last trace of magic and romance is beaten out of human existence, and the meaning of life is expressed in balances, deposits, percentages, and overdrafts--especially overdrafts. In a fine suite of rooms on the first floor of the bank building resides Mr. Lionel Woolley, the manager, with his wife May and their children. Mrs. Woolley is compelled to change her white window-curtains once a week because of the smuts. Mr. Woolley, forty-five, rather bald, frigidly suave, positive, egotistic, and pontifical, is a specimen of the man of business who is nothing else but a man of business. His career has been a calculation from which sentiment is entirely omitted; he has no instinct for the things which cannot be defined and assessed. Scarcely a manufacturer in Hanbridge but who inimically and fearfully regards Mr. Woolley as an amazing instance of a creature without a soul; and the absence of soul in a fellow-man must be very marked indeed before a Hanbridge manufacturer notices it. There are some sixty thousand immortal souls in Hanbridge, but they seldom attract attention.

Yet Mr. Woolley was once brought into contact with the things which cannot be defined and assessed; once he stood face to face with some strange visible resultant of those secret forces that lie beyond the human ken. And, moreover, the adventure affected the whole of his domestic life. The wonder and the pathos of the story lie in the fact that Nature, prodigal though she is known to be, should have wasted the rare and beautiful visitation on just Mr. Woolley. Mr. Woolley was bathed in romance of the most singular kind, and the precious fluid ran off him like water off a duck's back.

II

Ten years ago on a Thursday afternoon in July, Lionel Woolley, as he walked up through the new park at Bursley to his celibate rooms in Park Terrace, was making addition sums out of various items connected with the institution of marriage. Bursley is next door to Hanbridge, and Lionel happened then to be cashier of the Bursley branch of the bank.

He had in mind two possible wives, each of whom possessed advantages which appealed to him, and he was unable to decide between them by any mathematical process. Suddenly, from a glazed shelter near the empty bandstand, there emerged in front of him one of the delectable creatures who had excited his fancy. May Lawton was twenty-eight, an orphan, and a schoolmistress. She, too, had celibate rooms in Park Terrace, and it was owing to this coincidence that Lionel had made her acquaintance six months previously. She was not pretty, but she was tall, straight, well dressed, well educated, and not lacking in experience; and she had a little money of her own.

'Well, Mr. Woolley,' she said easily, stopping for him as she raised her sunshade, 'how satisfied you look!'

'It's the sight of you,' he replied, without a moment's hesitation.

He had a fine assured way with women (he need not have envied a curate accustomed to sewing meetings), and May Lawton belonged to the type of girl whose demeanour always challenges the masculine in a man. Gazing at her, Lionel was swiftly conscious of several things: the piquancy of her snub nose, the brightness of her smile, at once defiant and wistful, the lingering softness of her gloved hand, and the extraordinary charm of her sunshade, which matched her dress and formed a sort of canopy and frame for that intelligent, tantalizing face. He remembered that of late he and she had grown very intimate; and it came upon him with a shock, as though he had just opened a telegram which said so, that May, and not the other girl, was his destined mate. And he thought of her fortune, tiny but nevertheless useful, and how clever she was, and how inexplicably different from the rest of her sex, and how she would adorn his house, and set him off, and help him in his career. He heard himself saying negligently to friends: 'My wife speaks French like a native. Of course, my wife has travelled a great deal. My wife has thoroughly studied the management of children. Now, my wife does understand the art of dress. I put my wife's bit of money into so-and-so.' In short, Lionel was as near being in love as his character permitted.

And while he walked by May's side past the bowling-greens at the summit of the hill, she lightly quizzing the raw newness of the park and its appurtenances, he wondered, he honestly wondered, that he could ever have hesitated between May Lawton and the other. Her superiority was too obvious; she was a woman of the world! She.... In a flash he knew that he would propose to her that very afternoon. And when he had suggested a stroll towards Moorthorne, and she had deliciously agreed, he was conscious of a tumultuous uplifting and splendid carelessness of spirits. 'Imagine me bringing it to a climax to-day,' he reflected, profoundly pleased with himself. 'Ah well, it will be settled once for all!' He admired his own decision; he was quite struck by it. 'I shall call her May before I leave her,' he thought, gazing at her, and discovering how well the name suited her, with its significances of alertness, geniality, and half-mocking coyness.

'So school is closed,' he said, and added humorously: '"Broken up" is the technical term, I believe.'

'Yes,' she answered, 'and I had walked out into the park to meditate seriously upon the question of my holiday.'

She caught his eye in a net of bright glances, and romance was in the air. They had crossed a couple of smoke-soiled fields, and struck into the old Hanbridge road just below the abandoned toll-house with its broad eaves.

'And whither do your meditations point?' he demanded playfully.

'My meditations point to Switzerland,' she said. 'I have friends in Lausanne.'

The reference to foreign climes impressed him.

'Would that I could go to Switzerland too!' he exclaimed; and privately: 'Now for it! I'm about to begin.'

'Why?' she questioned, with elaborate simplicity.

At the moment, as they were passing the toll-house, the other girl appeared surprisingly from round the corner of the toll-house, where the lane from Toft End joins the highroad. This second creature was smaller than Miss Lawton, less assertive, less intelligent, perhaps, but much more beautiful.

Everyone halted and everyone blushed.

'May!' the interrupter at length stammered.

'May!' responded Miss Lawton lamely.

The other girl was named May too--May Deane, child of the well-known majolica manufacturer, who lived with his sons and daughter in a solitary and ancient house at Toft End.

Lionel Woolley said nothing until they had all shaken hands--his famous way with women seemed to have deserted him--and then he actually stated that he had forgotten an appointment, and must depart. He had gone before the girls could move.

When they were alone, the two Mays fronted each other, confused, hostile, almost homicidal.

'I hope I didn't spoil a tete-a-tete,' said May Deane, stiffly and sharply, in a manner quite foreign to her soft and yielding nature.

The schoolmistress, abandoning herself to an inexplicable but overwhelming impulse, took breath for a proud lie.

'No,' she answered; 'but if you had come three minutes earlier'

She smiled calmly.

'Oh!' murmured May Deane, after a pause.

III

That evening May Deane returned home at half-past nine. She had been with her two brothers to a lawn-tennis party at Hillport, and she told her father, who was reading the Staffordshire Signal in his accustomed solitude, that the boys were staying later for cards, but that she had declined to stay because she felt tired. She kissed the old widower good-night, and said that she should go to bed at once. But before retiring she visited the housekeeper in the kitchen in order to discuss certain household matters: Jim's early breakfast, the proper method of washing Herbert's new flannels (Herbert would be very angry if they were shrunk), and the dog-biscuits for Carlo. These questions settled, she went to her room, drew the blind, lighted some candles, and sat down near the window.

She was twenty-two, and she had about her that strange and charming nunlike mystery which often comes to a woman who lives alone and unguessed-at among male relatives.

Her room was her bower. No one, save the servants and herself, ever entered it. Mr. Deane and Jim and Bertie might glance carelessly through the open door in passing along the corridor, but had they chanced in idle curiosity to enter, the room would have struck them as unfamiliar, and they might perhaps have exclaimed with momentary interest, 'So this is May's room!' And some hint that May was more than a daughter and sister - a woman, withdrawn, secret, disturbing, living her own inner life side by side with the household life might have penetrated their obtuse paternal and fraternal masculinity. Her beautiful face (the nose and mouth were perfect, and at either extremity of the upper lip grew a soft down), her dark hair, her quiet voice and her gentle acquiescence (diversified by occasional outbursts of sarcasm), appealed to them and won them; but they accepted her as something of course, as something which went without saying. They adored her, and did not know that they adored her.

May took off her hat, stuck the pins into it again, and threw it on the bed, whose white and green counterpane hung down nearly to the floor on either side. Then she lay back in the chair, and, pulling away the blind, glanced through the window; the moon, rather dim behind the furnace lights of Red Cow Ironworks, was rising over Moorthorne. May dropped the blind with a wearied gesture, and turned within the room, examining its contents as if she had not seen them before: the wardrobe, the chest of drawers, which was also a dressing-table, the washstand, the dwarf book-case with its store of Edna Lyalls, Elizabeth Gaskells, Thackerays, Charlotte Yonges, Charlotte Brontes, a Thomas Hardy or so, and some old school-books. She looked at the pictures, including a sampler worked by a deceased aunt, at the loud-ticking Swiss clock on the mantelpiece, at the higgledy-piggledy photographs there, at the new Axminster carpet, the piece of linoleum in front of the washstand, and the bad joining of the wallpaper to the left of the door. She missed none of the details which she knew so well, with such long monotonous intimacy, and sighed.

Then she got up from the chair, and, opening a small drawer in the chest of drawers, put her hand familiarly to the back and drew forth a photograph. She carried the photograph to the light of the candles on the mantelpiece, and gazed at it attentively, puckering her brows. It was a portrait of Lionel Woolley. Heaven knows by what subterfuge or lucky accident she had obtained it, for Lionel certainly had not given it to her. She loved Lionel. She had loved him for five years, with a love silent, blind, intense, irrational, and too elemental to be concealed. Everyone knew of May's passion. Many women admired her taste; a few were shocked and puzzled by it. All the men of her acquaintance either pitied or despised her for it. Her father said nothing. Her brothers were less cautious, and summed up their opinion of Lionel in the curt, scornful assertion that he showed a tendency to cheat at tennis. But May would never hear ill of him; he was a god to her, and she could not hide her worship. For more than a year, until lately, she had been almost sure of him, and then came a faint vague rumour concerning Lionel and May Lawton, a rumour which she had refused to take seriously. The encounter of that afternoon, and Miss Lawton's triumphant remark, had dazed her. For seven hours she had existed in a kind of semi-conscious delirium, in which she could perceive nothing but the fatal fact, emerging more clearly every moment from the welter of her thoughts, that she had lost Lionel. Lionel had proposed to May Lawton, and been accepted, just before she surprised them together; and Lionel, with a man's excusable cowardice, had left his betrothed to announce the engagement.

She tore up the photograph, put the fragments in the grate, and set a light to them.

Her father's step sounded on the stairs; he hesitated, and knocked sharply at her door.

'What's burning, May?'

'It's all right, father,' she answered calmly, 'I'm only burning some papers in the fire-grate.'
'Well, see you don't burn the house down.'

He passed on.

Then she found a sheet of notepaper, and wrote on it in pencil, using the mantelpiece for a desk: 'Dear home. Good-night, good-bye.' She cogitated, and wrote further: 'Forgive me.--MAY.'

She put the message in an envelope, and wrote on the envelope 'Jim,' and placed it prominently in front of the clock. But after she had looked at it for a minute, she wrote 'Father' above Jim, and then 'Herbert' below.

There were noises in the hall; the boys had returned earlier than she expected. As they went along the corridor and caught a glimpse of her light under the door, Jim cried gaily: 'Now then, out with that light! A little thing like you ought to be asleep hours since.'

She listened for the bang of their door, and then, very hurriedly, she removed her pink frock and put on an old black one, which was rather tight in the waist. And she donned her hat, securing it carefully with both pins, extinguished the candles, and crept quietly downstairs, and so by the back-door into the garden. Carlo, the retriever, came halfway out of his kennel and greeted her in the moonlight with a yawn. She patted his head and ran stealthily up the garden, through the gate, and up the waste green land towards the crown of the hill.

IV

The top of Toft End is the highest land in the Five Towns, and from it may be clearly seen all the lurid evidences of manufacture which sweep across the borders of the sky on north, east, west, and south. North-eastwards lie the moorlands, and far off Manifold, the 'metropolis of the moorlands,' as it is called. On this night the furnaces of Red Cow Ironworks, in the hollow to the east, were in full blast; their fluctuating yellow light illuminated queerly the grass of the fields above Deane's house, and the regular roar of their breathing reached that solitary spot like the distant rumour of some leviathan beast angrily fuming. Further away to the south-west the Cauldon Bar Ironworks reproduced the same phenomena, and round the whole horizon, near and far, except to the north-east, the lesser fires of labour leapt and flickered and glinted in their mists of smoke, burning ceaselessly, as they burned every night and every day at all seasons of all years. The town of Bursley slept in the deep valley to the west, and vast Hanbridge in the shallower depression to the south, like two sleepers accustomed to rest quietly amid great disturbances; the beacons of their Town Halls and churches kept watch, and the whole scene was dominated by the placidity of the moon, which had now risen clear of the Red Cow furnace clouds, and was passing upwards through tracts of stars.

Into this scene, climbing up from the direction of Manifold, came Lionel Woolley, nearly at midnight, having walked some eighteen miles in a vain effort to re-establish his self-satisfaction by a process of reasoning and ingenious excuses. Lionel felt that in the brief episode of the afternoon he had scarcely behaved with dignity. In other words, he was fully and painfully aware that he must have looked a fool, a coward, an ass, a contemptible and pitiful person, in the eyes of at least one girl, if not of two. He did not like this, no man would have liked it; and to Lionel the memory of an undignified act was acute torture. Why had he bidden the girls adieu and departed? Why had he, in fact, run away? What precisely would May Lawton think of him? How could he explain his conduct to her and to himself? And had that worshipping, affectionate thing, May Deane, taken note of his confusion--of the confusion of him who was never confused, who was equal to every occasion and every emergency? These were some of the questions which harried him and declined to be settled. He had walked to Manifold, and had tea at the Roebuck, and walked back, and still the questions were harrying; and as he came over the hill by the field-path, and descried the lone house of the Deanes in the light of the Red Cow furnaces and of the moon, the worship of May Deane seemed suddenly very precious to him, and he could not bear to think that any stupidity of his should have impaired it.

Then he saw May Deane walking slowly across the field, close to an abandoned pit-shaft, whose low protecting circular wall of brick was crumbling to ruin on the side nearest to him.

She stopped, appeared to gaze at him intently, turned, and began to approach him. And he too, moved by a mysterious impulse which he did not pause to examine, swerved, and quickened his step in order to lessen the distance between them. He did not at first even feel surprise that she should be wandering solitary on the hill at that hour. Presently she stood still, while he continued to move forward. It was as if she drew him; and soon, in the pale moonlight and the wavering light of the furnaces, he could decipher all the details of her face, and he saw that she was smiling fondly, invitingly, admiringly, lustrously, with the old undiminished worship and affection. And he perceived a dark discoloration on her right cheek, as though she had suffered a blow, but this mark did not long occupy his mind. He thought suddenly of the strong probability that her father would leave a nice little bit of money to each of his three children; and he thought of her beauty, and of her timid fragility in the tight black dress, and of her immense and unquestioning love for him, which would survive all accidents and mishaps. He seemed to sink luxuriously into this grand passion of hers (which he deemed quite natural and proper) as into a soft feather-bed. To live secure in an atmosphere of exhaustless worship; to keep a fount of balm and admiration for ever in the house, a bubbling spring of passionate appreciation which would be continually available for the refreshment of his self-esteem! To be always sure of an obedience blind and willing, a subservience which no tyranny and no harshness and no whim would rouse into revolt; to sit on a throne with so much beauty kneeling at his feet!

And the possession of her beauty would be a source of legitimate pride to him. People would often refer to the beautiful Mrs. Woolley.

He felt that in sending May Deane to interrupt his highly emotional conversation with May Lawton Providence had watched over him and done him a good turn. May Lawton had advantages, and striking advantages, but he could not be sure of her. The suspicion that if she married him she would marry him for her own ends caused him a secret disquiet, and he feared that one day, perhaps one morning at breakfast, she might take it into her intelligent head to mock him, to exercise upon him her gift of irony, and to intimate to him that if he fancied she was his slave he was deceived. That she sincerely admired him he never for an instant doubted. But -

And, moreover, the unfortunate episode of the afternoon might have cooled her ardour to freezing-point.

He stood now in front of his worshipper, and the notion crossed his mind that in after-years he could say to his friends: 'I proposed to my wife at midnight under the moon. Not many men have done that.

'Good-evening,' he ventured to the girl; and he added with bravado: 'We've met before to-day, haven't we?'

She made no reply, but her smile was more affectionate, more inviting, than ever.

'I'm glad of this opportunity, very glad,' he proceeded. 'I've been wanting to ... You must know, my dear girl, how I feel....'

She gave a gesture, charming in its sweet humility, as if to say: 'Who am I that I should dare-'

And then he proposed to her, asked her to share his life, and all that sort of thing; and when he had finished he thought, 'It's done now, anyway.'

Strange to relate, she offered no immediate reply, but she bent a little towards him with shining, happy eyes. He had an impulse to seize her in his arms and kiss her, but prudence suggested that he should defer the rite. She turned and began to walk slowly and meditatively towards the pit-shaft. He followed almost at her side, but a foot or so behind, waiting for her to speak. And as he waited, expectant, he looked at her profile and reflected how well the name May suited her, with its significances of shyness and dreamy hope, and hidden fire and the modesty of spring.

And while he was thus savouring her face, and they were still ten yards from the pit-shaft, she suddenly disappeared from his vision, as it were by a conjuring trick. He had a horrible sensation in his spinal column. He was not the man to mistrust the evidence of his senses, and he knew, therefore, that he had been proposing to a phantom.

V

The next morning, early because of Jim's early breakfast, when May Deane's disappearance became known to the members of the household, Jim had the idea of utilizing Carlo in the search for her. The retriever went straight, without a fault, to the pit-shaft, and May was discovered alive and unscathed, save for a contusion of the face and a sprain in the wrist.

Her suicidal plunge had been arrested, at only a few feet from the top of the shaft, by a cross-stay of timber, upon which she lay prone. There was no reason why the affair should be made public, and it was not. It was suppressed into one of those secrets which embed themselves in the history of families, and after two or three generations blossom into romantic legends full of appropriate circumstantial detail.

Lionel Woolley spent a woeful night at his rooms. He did not know what to do, and on the following day May Lawton encountered him again, and proved by her demeanour that the episode of the previous afternoon had caused no estrangement. Lionel vacillated. The sway of the schoolmistress was almost restored, and it would have been restored fully had he not been preoccupied by a feverish curiosity -he curiosity to know whether or not May Deane was dead. He felt that she must indeed be dead, and he lived through the day expectant of the news of her sudden decease. Towards night his state of mind was such that he was obliged to call at the Deanes'. May heard him, and insisted on seeing him; more, she insisted on seeing him alone in the breakfast-room, where she reclined, interestingly white, on the sofa. Her father and brothers objected strongly to the interview, but they yielded, afraid that a refusal might induce hysteria and worse things.

And when Lionel Woolley came into the room, May, steeped in felicity, related to him the story of her impulsive crime.

'I was so happy,' she said, 'when I knew that Miss Lawton had deceived me.' And before he could inquire what she meant, she continued rapidly: 'I must have been unconscious, but I felt you were there, and something of me went out towards you. And oh! the answer to your question, I heard your question; the real me heard it, but that something could not speak.'
'My question?'

'You asked a question, didn't you?' she faltered, sitting up.

He hesitated, and then surrendered himself to her immense love and sank into it, and forgot May Lawton.

'Yes,' he said.

'The answer is yes. Oh, you must have known the answer would be yes! You did know, didn't you?'

He nodded grandly.

She sighed with delicious and overwhelming joy.

In the ecstasy of the achievement of her desire the girl gave little thought to the psychic aspect of the possibly unique wooing.

As for Lionel, he refused to dwell on it even in thought. And so that strange, magic, yearning effluence of a soul into a visible projection and shape was ignored, slurred over, and, after ten years of domesticity in the bank premises, is gradually being forgotten.

He is a man of business, and she, with her fading beauty, her ardent, continuous worship of the idol, her half-dozen small children, the eldest of whom is only eight, and the white window-curtains to change every week because of the smuts--do you suppose she has time or inclination to ponder upon the theory of the subliminal consciousness and kindred mysteries?

The Matador Of The Five Towns By Arnold Bennett

I

Mrs Brindeley looked across the lunch-table at her husband with glinting, eager eyes, which showed that there was something unusual in the brain behind them.

"Bob," she said, factitiously calm. "You don't know what I've just remembered!"

"Well?" said he.

"It's only grandma's birthday to-day!"

My friend Robert Brindley, the architect, struck the table with a violent fist, making his little boys blink, and then he said quietly:

"The deuce!"

I gathered that grandmamma's birthday had been forgotten and that it was not a festival that could be neglected with impunity. Both Mr and Mrs Brindley had evidently a humorous appreciation of crises, contretemps, and those collisions of circumstances which are usually called "junctures" for short. I could have imagined either of them saying to the other: "Here's a funny thing! The house is on fire!" And then yielding to laughter as they ran for buckets.

Mrs Brindley, in particular, laughed now; she gazed at the table-cloth and laughed almost silently to herself; though it appeared that their joint forgetfulness might result in temporary estrangement from a venerable ancestor who was also, birthdays being duly observed, a continual fount of rich presents in specie.

Robert Brindley drew a time-table from his breast-pocket with the rapid gesture of habit. All men of business in the Five Towns seem to carry that time-table in their breast-pockets. Then he examined his watch carefully.

"You'll have time to dress up your progeny and catch the 2.5. It makes the connection at Knype for Axe."

The two little boys, aged perhaps four and six, who had been ladling the messy contents of specially deep plates on to their bibs, dropped their spoons and began to babble about grea'-granny, and one of them insisted several times that he must wear his new gaiters.

"Yes," said Mrs Brindley to her husband, after reflection. "And a fine old crowd there'll be in the train--with this football match!"

"Can't be helped! Now, you kids, hook it upstairs to nurse."

"And what about you?" asked Mrs Brindley.

"You must tell the old lady I'm kept by business."

"I told her that last year, and you know what happened."

"Well," said Brindley. "Here Loring's just come. You don't expect me to leave him, do you? Or have you had the beautiful idea of taking him over to Axe to pass a pleasant Saturday afternoon with your esteemed grandmother?"

"No," said Mrs Brindley. "Hardly that!"

"Well, then?"

The boys, having first revolved on their axes, slid down from their high chairs as though from horses.

"Look here," I said. "You mustn't mind me. I shall be all right."

"Ha-ha!" shouted Brindley. "I seem to see you turned loose alone in this amusing town on a winter afternoon. I seem to see you!"

"I could stop in and read," I said, eyeing the multitudinous books on every wall of the dining-room. The house was dadoed throughout with books.

"Rot!" said Brindley.

This was only my third visit to his home and to the Five Towns, but he and I had already become curiously intimate. My first two visits had been occasioned by official pilgrimages as a British Museum expert in ceramics. The third was for a purely friendly week-end, and had no pretext. The fact is, I was drawn to the astonishing district and its astonishing inhabitants. The Five Towns, to me, was like the East to those who have smelt the East: it "called."

"I'll tell you what we could do," said Mrs Brindley. "We could put him on to Dr Stirling."

"So we could!" Brindley agreed. "Wife, this is one of your bright, intelligent days. We'll put you on to the doctor, Loring. I'll impress on him that he must keep you constantly amused till I get back, which I fear it won't be early. This is what we call manners, you know--to invite a fellow-creature to travel a hundred and fifty miles to spend two days here, and then to turn him out before he's been in the house an hour. It's us, that is! But the truth of the matter is, the birthday business might be a bit serious. It might easily cost me fifty quid and no end of diplomacy. If you were a married man you'd know that the ten plagues of Egypt are simply nothing in comparison with your wife's relations. And she's over eighty, the old lady."

"I'll give you ten plagues of Egypt!" Mrs Brindley menaced her spouse, as she wafted the boys from the room. "Mr Loring, do take some more of that cheese if you fancy it." She vanished.

Within ten minutes Brindley was conducting me to the doctor's, whose house was on the way to the station. In its spacious porch he explained the circumstances in six words, depositing me like a parcel. The doctor, who had once by mysterious medicaments saved my frail organism from the consequences of one of Brindley's Falstaffian "nights," hospitably protested his readiness to sacrifice patients to my pleasure.

"It'll be a chance for MacIlroy," said he.

"Who's MacIlroy?" I asked.

"MacIlroy is another Scotchman," growled Brindley. "Extraordinary how they stick together! When he wanted an assistant, do you suppose he looked about for some one in the district, some one who understood us and loved us and could take a hand at bridge? Not he! Off he goes to Cupar, or somewhere, and comes back with another stage Scotchman, named MacIlroy. Now listen here, Doc! A charge to keep you have, and mind you keep it, or I'll never pay your confounded bill. We'll knock on the window to-night as we come back. In the meantime you can show Loring your etchings, and pray for me." And to me: "Here's a latchkey." With no further ceremony he hurried away to join his wife and children at Bleakridge Station. In such singular manner was I transferred forcibly from host to host.

II

The doctor and I resembled each other in this: that there was no offensive affability about either of us. Though abounding in good-nature, we could not become intimate by a sudden act of volition. Our conversation was difficult, unnatural, and by gusts falsely familiar. He displayed to me his bachelor house, his etchings, a few specimens of modern rouge flambe ware made at Knype, his whisky, his celebrated prize-winning fox-terrier Titus, the largest collection of books in the Five Towns, and photographs of Marischal College, Aberdeen. Then we fell flat, socially prone. Sitting in his study, with Titus between us on the hearthrug, we knew no more what to say or do. I regretted that Brindley's wife's grandmother should have been born on a fifteenth of February. Brindley was a vivacious talker, he could be trusted to talk. I, too, am a good talker--with another good talker. With a bad talker I am just a little worse than he is. The doctor said abruptly after a nerve-trying silence that he had forgotten a most important call at Hanbridge, and would I care to go with him in the car? I was and still am convinced that he was simply inventing.
He wanted to break the sinister spell by getting out of the house, and he had not the face to suggest a sortie into the streets of the Five Towns as a promenade of pleasure.

So we went forth, splashing warily through the rich mud and the dank mist of Trafalgar Road, past all those strange little Indian-red houses, and ragged empty spaces, and poster-hoardings, and rounded kilns, and high, smoking chimneys, up hill, down hill, and up hill again, encountering and overtaking many electric trams that dipped and rose like ships at sea, into Crown Square, the centre of Hanbridge, the metropolis of the Five Towns. And while the doctor paid his mysterious call I stared around me at the large shops and the banks and the gilded hotels. Down the radiating street-vistas I could make out the facades of halls, theatres, chapels. Trams rumbled continually in and out of the square. They seemed to enter casually, to hesitate a few moments as if at a loss, and then to decide with a nonchalant clang of bells that they might as well go off somewhere else in search of something more interesting. They were rather like human beings who are condemned to live forever in a place of which they are sick beyond the expressiveness of words.

And indeed the influence of Crown Square, with its large effects of terra cotta, plate glass, and gold letters, all under a heavy skyscape of drab smoke, was depressing. A few very seedy men (sharply contrasting with the fine delicacy of costly things behind plate-glass) stood doggedly here and there in the mud, immobilized by the gloomy enchantment of the Square. Two of them turned to look at Stirling's motor-car and me. They gazed fixedly for a long time, and then one said, only his lips moving:

"Has Tommy stood thee that there quart o' beer as he promised thee?"

No reply, no response of any sort, for a further long period! Then the other said, with grim resignation:

"Ay!"

The conversation ceased, having made a little oasis in the dismal desert of their silent scrutiny of the car. Except for an occasional stamp of the foot they never moved. They just doggedly and indifferently stood, blown upon by all the nipping draughts of the square, and as it might be sinking deeper and deeper into its dejection. As for me, instead of desolating, the harsh disconsolateness of the scene seemed to uplift me; I savoured it with joy, as one savours the melancholy of a tragic work of art.

"We might go down to the Signal offices and worry Buchanan a bit," said the doctor, cheerfully, when he came back to the car. This was the second of his inspirations.

Buchanan, of whom I had heard, was another Scotchman and the editor of the sole daily organ of the Five Towns, an evening newspaper cried all day in the streets and read by the entire population. Its green sheet appeared to be a permanent waving feature of the main thoroughfares. The offices lay round a corner close by, and as we drew up in front of them a crowd of tattered urchins interrupted their diversions in the sodden road to celebrate our glorious arrival by unanimously yelling at the top of their strident and hoarse voices:

"Hooray! Hoo-blooody-ray!"

Abashed, I followed my doctor into the shelter of the building, a new edifice, capacious and considerable, but horribly faced with terra cotta, and quite unimposing, lacking in the spectacular effect; like nearly everything in the Five Towns, carelessly and scornfully ugly!
The mean, swinging double-doors returned to the assault when you pushed them, and hit you viciously. In a dark, countered room marked "Enquiries" there was nobody.

"Hi, there!" called the doctor.

A head appeared at a door.

"Mr Buchanan upstairs?"

"Yes," snapped the head, and disappeared.

Up a dark staircase we went, and at the summit were half flung back again by another self-acting door.

In the room to which we next came an old man and a youngish one were bent over a large, littered table, scribbling on and arranging pieces of grey tissue paper and telegrams. Behind the old man stood a boy. Neither of them looked up.

"Mr Buchanan in his" the doctor began to question. "Oh! There you are!"

The editor was standing in hat and muffler at the window, gazing out. His age was about that of the doctor, forty or so; and like the doctor he was rather stout and clean-shaven. Their Scotch accents mingled in greeting, the doctor's being the more marked. Buchanan shook my hand with a certain courtliness, indicating that he was well accustomed to receive strangers. As an expert in small talk, however, he shone no brighter than his visitors, and the three of us stood there by the window awkwardly in the heaped disorder of the room, while the other two men scratched and fidgeted with bits of paper at the soiled table.

Suddenly and savagely the old man turned on the boy:

"What the hades are you waiting there for?"

"I thought there was something else, sir."

"Sling your hook."

Buchanan winked at Stirling and me as the boy slouched off and the old man blandly resumed his writing.

"Perhaps you'd like to look over the place?" Buchanan suggested politely to me. "I'll come with you. It's all I'm fit for to-day.... 'Flu!" He glanced at Stirling, and yawned.

"Ye ought to be in bed," said Stirling.

"Yes. I know. I've known it for twelve years. I shall go to bed as soon as I get a bit of time to myself. Well, will you come? The half-time results are beginning to come in."

A telephone-bell rang impatiently.

"You might just see what that is, boss," said the old man without looking up.

Buchanan went to the telephone and replied into it: "Yes? What? Oh! Myatt? Yes, he's playing.... Of course I'm sure! Good-bye." He turned to the old man: "It's another of 'em wanting to know if Myatt is playing. Birmingham, this time."

"Ah!" exclaimed the old man, still writing.

"It's because of the betting," Buchanan glanced at me. "The odds are on Knype now, three to two."

"If Myatt is playing Knype have got me to thank for it," said the doctor, surprisingly.

"You?"

"Me! He fetched me to his wife this morning. She's nearing her confinement. False alarm. I guaranteed him at least another twelve hours."

"Oh! So that's it, is it?" Buchanan murmured.

Both the sub-editors raised their heads.

"That's it," said the doctor.

"Some people were saying he'd quarrelled with the trainer again and was shamming," said Buchanan. "But I didn't believe that. There's no hanky-panky about Jos Myatt, anyhow."

I learnt in answer to my questions that a great and terrible football match was at that moment in progress at Knype, a couple of miles away, between the Knype Club and the Manchester Rovers. It was conveyed to me that the importance of this match was almost national, and that the entire district was practically holding its breath till the result should be known. The half-time result was one goal each.

"If Knype lose," said Buchanan, explanatorily, "they'll find themselves pushed out of the First League at the end of the season. That's a cert ... one of the oldest clubs in England! Semi-finalists for the English Cup in '78."

"'79," corrected the elder sub-editor.

I gathered that the crisis was grave.

"And Myatt's the captain, I suppose?" said I.

"No. But he's the finest full-back in the League."

I then had a vision of Myatt as a great man. By an effort of the imagination I perceived that the equivalent of the fate of nations depended upon him. I recollected, now, large yellow posters on the hoardings we had passed, with the names of Knype and of Manchester Rovers in letters a foot high and the legend "League match at Knype" over all. It seemed to me that the heroic name of Jos Myatt, if truly he were the finest full-back in the League, if truly his presence or absence affected the betting as far off as Birmingham, ought also to have been on the posters, together with possibly his portrait. I saw Jos Myatt as a matador, with a long ribbon of scarlet necktie down his breast, and embroidered trousers.

"Why," said Buchanan, "if Knype drop into the Second Division they'll never pay another dividend! It'll be all up with first-class football in the Five Towns!"

The interests involved seemed to grow more complicated. And here I had been in the district nearly four hours without having guessed that the district was quivering in the tense excitement of gigantic issues! And here was this Scotch doctor, at whose word the great Myatt would have declined to play, never saying a syllable about the affair, until a chance remark from Buchanan loosened his tongue. But all doctors are strangely secretive. Secretiveness is one of their chief private pleasures.

"Come and see the pigeons, eh?" said Buchanan.

"Pigeons?" I repeated.

"We give the results of over a hundred matches in our Football Edition," said Buchanan, and added: "not counting Rugby."

As we left the room two boys dodged round us into it, bearing telegrams.

In a moment we were, in the most astonishing manner, on a leaden roof of the Signal offices. High factory chimneys rose over the horizon of slates on every side, blowing thick smoke into the general murk of the afternoon sky, and crossing the western crimson with long pennons of black. And out of the murk there came from afar a blue-and-white pigeon which circled largely several times over the offices of the Signal. At length it descended, and I could hear the whirr of its strong wings. The wings ceased to beat and the pigeon slanted downwards in a curve, its head lower than its wide tail. Then the little head gradually rose and the tail fell; the curve had changed, the pace slackened; the pigeon was calculating with all its brain; eyes, wings, tail and feet were being co-ordinated to the resolution of an intricate mechanical problem. The pinkish claws seemed to grope--and after an instant of hesitation the thing was done, the problem solved; the pigeon, with delicious gracefulness, had established equilibrium on the ridge of a pigeon-cote, and folded its wings, and was peering about with strange motions of its extremely movable head. Presently it flew down to the leads, waddled to and fro with the ungainly gestures of a fat woman of sixty, and disappeared into the cote. At the same moment the boy who had been dismissed from the sub-editor's room ran forward and entered the cote by a wire-screened door.

"Handy things, pigeons!" said the doctor as we approached to examine the cote. Fifty or sixty pigeons were cooing and strutting in it. There was a protest of wings as the boy seized the last arriving messenger.

"Give it here!" Buchanan ordered.

The boy handed over a thin tube of paper which he had unfastened from the bird's leg. Buchanan unrolled it and showed it to me. I read: "Midland Federation. Axe United, Macclesfield Town. Match abandoned after half-hour's play owing to fog. Three forty-five."

"Three forty-five," said Buchanan, looking at his watch. "He's done the ten miles in half an hour, roughly. Not bad. First time we tried pigeons from as far off as Axe. Here, boy!" And he restored the paper to the boy, who gave it to another boy, who departed with it.

"Man," said the doctor, eyeing Buchanan. "Ye'd no business out here. Ye're not precisely a pigeon."

Down we went, one after another, by the ladder, and now we fell into the composing-room, where Buchanan said he felt warmer. An immense, dirty, white-washed apartment crowded with linotypes and other machines, in front of which sat men in white aprons, tapping, tapping; gazing at documents pinned at the level of their eyes--and tapping, tapping. A kind of cavernous retreat in which monstrous iron growths rose out of the floor and were met half-way by electric flowers that had their roots in the ceiling! In this jungle there was scarcely room for us to walk. Buchanan explained the linotypes to me. I watched, as though romantically dreaming, the flashing descent of letter after letter, a rain of letters into the belly of the machine; then, going round to the back, I watched the same letters rising again in a close, slow procession, and sorting themselves by themselves at the top in readiness to answer again to the tapping, tapping of a man in a once-white apron. And while I was watching all that I could somehow, by a faculty which we have, at the same time see pigeons far overhead, arriving and arriving out of the murk from beyond the verge of chimneys.

"Ingenious, isn't it?" said Stirling.

But I imagine that he had not the faculty by which to see the pigeons.

A reverend, bearded, spectacled man, with his shirt-sleeves rolled up and an apron stretched over his hemispherical paunch, strolled slowly along an alley, glancing at a galley-proof with an ingenuous air just as if he had never seen a galley-proof before.

"It's a stick more than a column already," said he confidentially, offering the long paper, and then gravely looking at Buchanan, with head bent forward, not through his spectacles but over them.

37

The editor negligently accepted the proof, and I read a series of titles: "Knype v. Manchester Rovers. Record Gate. Fifteen thousand spectators. Two goals in twelve minutes. Myatt in form. Special Report."

Buchanan gave the slip back without a word.

"There you are!" said he to me, as another compositor near us attached a piece of tissue paper to his machine. It was the very paper that I had seen come out of the sky, but its contents had been enlarged and amended by the sub-editorial pen. The man began tapping, tapping, and the letters began to flash downwards on their way to tell a quarter of a million people that Axe v. Macclesfield had been stopped by fog.

"I suppose that Knype match is over by now?" I said.

"Oh no!" said Buchanan. "The second half has scarcely begun."

"Like to go?" Stirling asked.

"Well," I said, feeling adventurous, "it's a notion, isn't it?"

"You can run Mr Loring down there in five or six minutes," said Buchanan. "And he's probably never seen anything like it before. You might call here as you come home and see the paper on the machines."

III

We went on the Grand Stand, which was packed with men whose eyes were fixed, with an unconscious but intense effort, on a common object. Among the men were a few women in furs and wraps, equally absorbed. Nobody took any notice of us as we insinuated our way up a rickety flight of wooden stairs, but when by misadventure we grazed a human being the elbow of that being shoved itself automatically and fiercely outwards, to repel. I had an impression of hats, caps, and woolly overcoats stretched in long parallel lines, and of grimy raw planks everywhere presenting possibly dangerous splinters, save where use had worn them into smooth shininess. Then gradually I became aware of the vast field, which was more brown than green. Around the field was a wide border of infinitesimal hats and pale faces, rising in tiers, and beyond this border fences, hoardings, chimneys, furnaces, gasometers, telegraph-poles, houses, and dead trees. And here and there, perched in strange perilous places, even high up towards the sombre sky, were more human beings clinging. On the field itself, at one end of it, were a scattered handful of doll-like figures, motionless; some had white bodies, others red; and three were in black; all were so small and so far off that they seemed to be mere unimportant casual incidents in whatever recondite affair it was that was proceeding. Then a whistle shrieked, and all these figures began simultaneously to move, and then I saw a ball in the air. An obscure, uneasy murmuring rose from the immense multitude like an invisible but audible vapour. The next instant the vapour had condensed into a sudden shout. Now I saw the ball rolling solitary in the middle of the field, and a single red doll racing towards it; at one end was a confused group of red and white, and at the other two white dolls, rather lonely in the expanse. The single red doll overtook the ball and scudded along with it at his twinkling toes. A great voice behind me bellowed with an incredible volume of sound:

"Now, Jos!"

And another voice, further away, bellowed:

"Now, Jos!"

And still more distantly the grim warning shot forth from the crowd:

"Now, Jos! Now, Jos!"

The nearer of the white dolls, as the red one approached, sprang forward. I could see a leg. And the ball was flying back in a magnificent curve into the skies; it passed out of my sight, and then I heard a bump on the slates of the roof of the grand stand, and it fell among the crowd in the stand-enclosure. But almost before the flight of the ball had commenced, a terrific roar of relief had rolled formidably round the field, and out of that roar, like rockets out of thick smoke, burst acutely ecstatic cries of adoration:

"Bravo, Jos!"

"Good old Jos!"

The leg had evidently been Jos's leg. The nearer of these two white dolls must be Jos, darling of fifteen thousand frenzied people.

Stirling punched a neighbour in the side to attract his attention.

"What's the score?" he demanded of the neighbour, who scowled and then grinned. "Two-one-agen uz!" The other growled.

"It'll take our balls all their time to draw. They're playing a man short."

"Accident?"

"No! Referee ordered him off for rough play."

Several spectators began to explain, passionately, furiously, that the referee's action was utterly bereft of common sense and justice; and I gathered that a less gentlemanly crowd would undoubtedly have lynched the referee. The explanations died down, and everybody except me resumed his fierce watch on the field.

I was recalled from the exercise of a vague curiosity upon the set, anxious faces around me by a crashing, whooping cheer which in volume and sincerity of joy surpassed all noises in my experience. This massive cheer reverberated round the field like the echoes of a battleship's broadside in a fiord. But it was human, and therefore more terrible than guns. I instinctively thought: "If such are the symptoms of pleasure, what must be the symptoms of pain or disappointment?" Simultaneously with the expulsion of the unique noise the expression of the faces changed. Eyes sparkled; teeth became prominent in enormous, uncontrolled smiles. Ferocious satisfaction had to find vent in ferocious gestures, wreaked either upon dead wood or upon the living tissues of fellow-creatures. The gentle, mannerly sound of hand-clapping was a kind of light froth on the surface of the billowy sea of heartfelt applause. The host of the fifteen thousand might have just had their lives saved, or their children snatched from destruction and their wives from dishonour; they might have been preserved from bankruptcy, starvation, prison, torture; they might have been rewarding with their impassioned worship a band of national heroes. But it was not so. All that had happened was that the ball had rolled into the net of the Manchester Rovers' goal. Knype had drawn level. The reputation of the Five Towns before the jury of expert opinion that could distinguish between first-class football and second-class was maintained intact. I could hear specialists around me proving that though Knype had yet five League matches to play, its situation was safe. They pointed excitedly to a huge hoarding at one end of the ground on which appeared names of other clubs with changing figures. These clubs included the clubs which Knype would have to meet before the end of the season, and the figures indicated their fortunes on various grounds similar to this ground all over the country. If a goal was scored in Newcastle, or in Southampton, the very Peru of first-class football, it was registered on that board and its possible effect on the destinies of Knype was instantly assessed. The calculations made were dizzying.

Then a little flock of pigeons flew up and separated, under the illusion that they were free agents and masters of the air, but really wafted away to fixed destinations on the stupendous atmospheric waves of still-continued cheering.

After a minute or two the ball was restarted, and the greater noise had diminished to the sensitive uneasy murmur which responded like a delicate instrument to the fluctuations of the game. Each feat and manoeuvre of Knype drew generous applause in proportion to its intention or its success, and each sleight of the Manchester Rovers, successful or not, provoked a holy disgust. The attitude of the host had passed beyond morality into religion.

Then, again, while my attention had lapsed from the field, a devilish, a barbaric, and a deafening yell broke from those fifteen thousand passionate hearts. It thrilled me; it genuinely frightened me. I involuntarily made the motion of swallowing. After the thunderous crash of anger from the host came the thin sound of a whistle. The game stopped. I heard the same word repeated again and again, in divers tones of exasperated fury:

"Foul!"

I felt that I was hemmed in by potential homicides, whose arms were lifted in the desire of murder and whose features were changed from the likeness of man into the corporeal form of some pure and terrible instinct.

And I saw a long doll rise from the ground and approach a lesser doll with threatening hands.

"Foul! Foul!"

"Go it, Jos! Knock his neck out! Jos! He tripped thee up!"

There was a prolonged gesticulatory altercation between the three black dolls in leather leggings and several of the white and the red dolls. At last one of the mannikins in leggings shrugged his shoulders, made a definite gesture to the other two, and walked away towards the edge of the field nearest the stand. It was the unprincipled referee; he had disallowed the foul. In the protracted duel between the offending Manchester forward and the great, honest Jos Myatt he had given another point to the enemy. As soon as the host realized the infamy it yelled once more in heightened fury. It seemed to surge in masses against the thick iron railings that alone stood between the referee and death. The discreet referee was approaching the grand stand as the least unsafe place. In a second a handful of executioners had somehow got on to the grass. And in the next second several policemen were in front of them, not striking nor striving to intimidate, but heavily pushing them into bounds.

40

"Get back there!" cried a few abrupt, commanding voices from the stand.

The referee stood with his hands in his pockets and his whistle in his mouth. I think that in that moment of acutest suspense the whole of his earthly career must have flashed before him in a phantasmagoria. And then the crisis was past. The inherent gentlemanliness of the outraged host had triumphed and the referee was spared.

"Served him right if they'd man-handled him!" said a spectator.

"Ay!" said another, gloomily, "ay! And th' Football Association 'ud ha' fined us maybe a hundred quid and disqualified th' ground for the rest o' th' season!"

"Down th' Football Association!"

"Ay! But you canna'!"

"Now, lads! Play up, Knype! Now, lads! Give 'em hot hell!" Different voices heartily encouraged the home team as the ball was thrown into play.

The fouling Manchester forward immediately resumed possession of the ball. Experience could not teach him. He parted with the ball and got it again, twice. The devil was in him and in the ball. The devil was driving him towards Myatt. They met. And then came a sound quite new: a cracking sound, somewhat like the snapping of a bough, but sharper, more decisive.

"By Jove!" exclaimed Stirling. "That's his bone!"

And instantly he was off down the staircase and I after him. But he was not the first doctor on the field. Nothing had been unforeseen in the wonderful organization of this enterprise. A pigeon sped away and an official doctor and an official stretcher appeared, miraculously, simultaneously. It was tremendous. It inspired awe in me.

"He asked for it!" I heard a man say as I hesitated on the shore of the ocean of mud.

Then I knew that it was Manchester and not Knype that had suffered. The confusion and hubbub were in a high degree disturbing and puzzling. But one emotion emerged clear: pleasure. I felt it myself. I was aware of joy in that the two sides were now levelled to ten men apiece. I was mystically identified with the Five Towns, absorbed into their life. I could discern on every face the conviction that a divine providence was in this affair, that God could not be mocked. I too had this conviction. I could discern also on every face the fear lest the referee might give a foul against the hero Myatt, or even order him off the field, though of course the fracture was a simple accident. I too had this fear. It was soon dispelled by the news which swept across the entire enclosure like a sweet smell, that the referee had adopted the theory of a simple accident. I saw vaguely policemen, a stretcher, streaming crowds, and my ears heard a monstrous universal babbling. And then the figure of Stirling detached itself from the moving disorder and came to me.

"Well, Hyatt's calf was harder than the other chap's, that's all," he said.

"Which is Myatt?" I asked, for the red and the white dolls had all vanished at close quarters, and were replaced by unrecognizably gigantic human animals, still clad, however, in dolls' vests and dolls' knickerbockers.

Stirling warningly jerked his head to indicate a man not ten feet away from me. This was Myatt, the hero of the host and the darling of populations. I gazed up at him. His mouth and his left knee were red with blood, and he was piebald with thick patches of mud from his tousled crown to his enormous boot. His blue eyes had a heavy, stupid, honest glance; and of the three qualities stupidity predominated. He seemed to be all feet, knees, hands and elbows. His head was very small--the sole remainder of the doll in him.

A little man approached him, conscious somewhat too obviously conscious of his right to approach. Myatt nodded.

"Ye'n settled him, seemingly, Jos!" said the little man.

"Well," said Myatt, with slow bitterness. "Hadn't he been blooming well begging and praying for it, aw afternoon? Hadn't he now?"

The little man nodded. Then he said in a lower tone:

"How's missis, like?"

"Her's altogether yet," said Myatt. "Or I'd none ha' played!"

"I've bet Watty half-a-dollar as it inna' a lad!" said the little man.

Myatt seemed angry.

"Wilt bet me half a quid as it inna' a lad?" he demanded, bending down and scowling and sticking out his muddy chin.

"Ay!" said the little man, not blenching.

"Evens?"

"Evens."

"I'll take thee, Charlie," said Myatt, resuming his calm.

The whistle sounded. And several orders were given to clear the field. Eight minutes had been lost over a broken leg, but Stirling said that the referee would surely deduct them from the official time, so that after all the game would not be shortened.

"I'll be up yon, to-morra morning," said the little man.

Myatt nodded and departed. Charlie, the little man, turned on his heel and proudly rejoined the crowd. He had been seen of all in converse with supreme greatness.

Stirling and I also retired; and though Jos Myatt had not even done his doctor the honour of seeing him, neither of us, I think, was quite without a consciousness of glory: I cannot imagine why. The rest of the game was flat and tame. Nothing occurred. The match ended in a draw.

IV

We were swept from the football ground on a furious flood of humanity, carried forth and flung down a slope into a large waste space that separated the ground from the nearest streets of little reddish houses. At the bottom of the slope, on my suggestion, we halted for a few moments aside, while the current rushed forward and, spreading out, inundated the whole space in one marvellous minute. The impression of the multitude streaming from that gap in the wooden wall was like nothing more than the impression of a burst main which only the emptying of the reservoir will assuage. Anybody who wanted to commit suicide might have stood in front of that gap and had his wish. He would not have been noticed. The interminable and implacable infantry charge would have passed unheedingly over him. A silent, preoccupied host, bent on something else now, and perhaps teased by the inconvenient thought that after all a draw is not as good as a win! It hurried blindly, instinctively outwards, knees and chins protruding, hands deep in pockets, chilled feet stamping. Occasionally someone stopped or slackened to light a pipe, and on being curtly bunted onward by a blind force from behind, accepted the hint as an atom accepts the law of gravity. The fever and ecstasy were over. What fascinated the Southern in me was the grim taciturnity, the steady stare (vacant or dreaming), and the heavy, muffled, multitudinous tramp shaking the cindery earth. The flood continued to rage through the gap.

Our automobile had been left at the Haycock Hotel; we went to get it, braving the inundation. Nearly opposite the stable-yard the electric trams started for Hanbridge, Bursley and Turnhill, and for Longshaw. Here the crowd was less dangerous, but still very formidable to my eyes. Each tram as it came up was savagely assaulted, seized, crammed and possessed, with astounding rapidity. Its steps were the western bank of a Beresina. At a given moment the inured conductor, brandishing his leather-shielded arm with a pitiless gesture, thrust aspirants down into the mud and the tram rolled powerfully away. All this in silence.

After a few minutes a bicyclist swished along through the mud, taking the far side of the road, which was comparatively free. He wore grey trousers, heavy boots, and a dark cut-away coat, up the back of which a line of caked mud had deposited itself. On his head was a bowler hat.

"How do, Jos?" cried a couple of boys, cheekily. And then there were a few adult greetings of respect.

It was the hero, in haste.

"Out of it, there!" he warned impeders, between his teeth, and plugged on with bent head.

"He keeps the Foaming Quart up at Toft End," said the doctor. "It's the highest pub in the Five Towns. He used to be what they call a pot-hunter, a racing bicyclist, you know. But he's got past that and he'll soon be past football. He's thirty-four if he's a day. That's one reason why he's so independent--that and because he's almost the only genuine native in the team."

"Why?" I asked. "Where do they come from, then?"

"Oh!" said Stirling as he gently started the car. "The club buys 'em, up and down the country. Four of 'em are Scots. A few years ago an Oldham club offered Knype L500 for Myatt, a big price--more than he's worth now! But he wouldn't go, though they guaranteed to put him into a first-class pub--a free house. He's never cost Knype anything except his wages and the goodwill of the Foaming Quart."

"What are his wages?"

"Don't know exactly. Not much. The Football Association fix a maximum. I daresay about four pounds a week Hi there! Are you deaf?"

"Thee mind what tha'rt about!" responded a stout loiterer in our path. "Or I'll take thy ears home for my tea, mester."

Stirling laughed.

In a few minutes we had arrived at Hanbridge, splashing all the way between two processions that crowded either footpath. And in the middle of the road was a third procession of trams,--tram following tram, each gorged with passengers, frothing at the step with passengers; not the lackadaisical trams that I had seen earlier in the afternoon in Crown Square; a different race of trams, eager and impetuous velocities. We reached the Signal offices. No crowd of urchins to salute us this time!

Under the earth was the machine-room of the Signal. It reminded me of the bowels of a ship, so full was it of machinery. One huge machine clattered slowly, and a folded green thing dropped strangely on to a little iron table in front of us. Buchanan opened it, and I saw that the broken leg was in it at length, together with a statement that in the Signal's opinion the sympathy of every true sportsman would be with the disabled player. I began to say something to Buchanan, when suddenly I could not hear my own voice. The great machine, with another behind us, was working at a fabulous speed and with a fabulous clatter. All that my startled senses could clearly disentangle was that the blue arc-lights above us blinked occasionally, and that folded green papers were snowing down upon the iron table far faster than the eye could follow them.

Tall lads in aprons elbowed me away and carried off the green papers in bundles, but not more quickly than the machine shed them. Buchanan put his lips to my ear. But I could hear nothing. I shook my head. He smiled, and led us out from the tumult.

"Come and see the boys take them," he said at the foot of the stairs.

In a sort of hall on the ground floor was a long counter, and beyond the counter a system of steel railings in parallel lines, so arranged that a person entering at the public door could only reach the counter by passing up or down each alley in succession. These steel lanes, which absolutely ensured the triumph of right over might, were packed with boys--the ragged urchins whom we had seen playing in the street. But not urchins now; rather young tigers! Perhaps half a dozen had reached the counter; the rest were massed behind, shouting and quarrelling. Through a hole in the wall, at the level of the counter, bundles of papers shot continuously, and were snatched up by servers, who distributed them in smaller bundles to the hungry boys; who flung down metal discs in exchange and fled, fled madly as though fiends were after them, through a third door, out of the pandemonium into the darkling street. And unceasingly the green papers appeared at the hole in the wall and unceasingly they were plucked away and borne off by those maddened children, whose destination was apparently Aix or Ghent, and whose wings were their tatters.

"What are those discs?" I inquired.

"The lads have to come and buy them earlier in the day," said Buchanan. "We haven't time to sell this edition for cash, you see."

"Well," I said as we left, "I'm very much obliged."

"What on earth for?" Buchanan asked.

"Everything," I said.

We returned through the squares of Hanbridge and by Trafalgar Road to Stirling's house at Bleakridge. And everywhere in the deepening twilight I could see the urchins, often hatless and sometimes scarcely shod, scudding over the lamp-reflecting mire with sheets of wavy green, and above the noises of traffic I could hear the shrill outcry: "Signal. Football Edition. Football Edition. Signal." The world was being informed of the might of Jos Myatt, and of the averting of disaster from Knype, and of the results of over a hundred other matches--not counting Rugby.

V

During the course of the evening, when Stirling had thoroughly accustomed himself to the state of being in sole charge of an expert from the British Museum, London, and the high walls round his more private soul had yielded to my timid but constant attacks, we grew fairly intimate. And in particular the doctor proved to me that his reputation for persuasive raciness with patients was well founded. Yet up to the time of dessert I might have been justified in supposing that that much-praised "manner" in a sick-room was nothing but a provincial legend. Such may be the influence of a quite inoffensive and shy Londoner in the country. At half-past ten, Titus being already asleep for the night in an arm-chair, we sat at ease over the fire in the study telling each other stories. We had dealt with the arts, and with medicine; now we were dealing with life, in those aspects of it which cause men to laugh and women uneasily to wonder. Once or twice we had mentioned the Brindleys. The hour for their arrival was come. But being deeply comfortable and content where I was, I felt no impatience. Then there was a tap on the window.
"That's Bobbie!" said Stirling, rising slowly from his chair. "He won't refuse whisky, even if you do. I'd better get another bottle."

The tap was repeated peevishly.

"I'm coming, laddie!" Stirling protested.

He slippered out through the hall and through the surgery to the side door, I following, and Titus sneezing and snuffing in the rear.

"I say, mester," said a heavy voice as the doctor opened the door. It was not Brindley, but Jos Myatt. Unable to locate the bell-push in the dark, he had characteristically attacked the sole illuminated window. He demanded, or he commanded, very curtly, that the doctor should go up instantly to the Foaming Quart at Toft End.

Stirling hesitated a moment.

"All right, my man," said he, calmly.

"Now?" the heavy, suspicious voice on the doorstep insisted.

"I'll be there before ye if ye don't sprint, man. I'll run up in the car." Stirling shut the door. I heard footsteps on the gravel path outside.

"Ye heard?" said he to me. "And what am I to do with ye?"

"I'll go with you, of course," I answered.

"I may be kept up there a while."

"I don't care," I said roisterously. "It's a pub and I'm a traveller."

Stirling's household was in bed and his assistant gone home. While he and Titus got out the car I wrote a line for the Brindleys: "Gone with doctor to see patient at Toft End. Don't wait up. A.L." This we pushed under Brindley's front door on our way forth. Very soon we were vibrating up a steep street on the first speed of the car, and the yellow reflections of distant furnaces began to shine over house roofs below us. It was exhilaratingly cold, a clear and frosty night, tonic, bracing after the enclosed warmth of the study. I was joyous, but silently. We had quitted the kingdom of the god Pan; we were in Lucina's realm, its consequence, where there is no laughter. We were on a mission.

"I didn't expect this," said Stirling.

"No?" I said. "But seeing that he fetched you this morning"

"Oh! That was only in order to be sure, for himself. His sister was there, in charge. Seemed very capable. Knew all about everything. Until ye get to the high social status of a clerk or a draper's assistant people seem to manage to have their children without professional assistance."

"Then do you think there's anything wrong?" I asked.

"I'd not be surprised."
He changed to the second speed as the car topped the first bluff. We said no more. The night and the mission solemnized us. And gradually, as we rose towards the purple skies, the Five Towns wrote themselves out in fire on the irregular plain below.

"That's Hanbridge Town Hall," said Stirling, pointing to the right. "And that's Bursley Town Hall," he said, pointing to the left. And there were many other beacons, dominating the jewelled street-lines that faded on the horizon into golden-tinted smoke.

The road was never quite free of houses. After occurring but sparsely for half a mile, they thickened into a village--the suburb of Bursley called Toft End. I saw a moving red light in front of us. It was the reverse of Hyatt's bicycle lantern. The car stopped near the dark facade of the inn, of which two yellow windows gleamed. Stirling, under Myatt's shouted guidance, backed into an obscure yard under cover. The engine ceased to throb.

"Friend of mine," he introduced me to Myatt. "By the way, Loring, pass me my bag, will you? Mustn't forget that." Then he extinguished the acetylene lamps, and there was no light in the yard except the ray of the bicycle lantern which Myatt held in his hand. We groped towards the house. Strange, every step that I take in the Five Towns seems to have the genuine quality of an adventure!

VI
In five minutes I was of no account in the scheme of things at Toft End, and I began to wonder why I had come. Stirling, my sole protector, had vanished up the dark stairs of the house, following a stout, youngish woman in a white apron, who bore a candle. Jos Myatt, behind, said to me: "Happen you'd better go in there, mester," pointing to a half-open door at the foot of the stairs. I went into a little room at the rear of the bar-parlour. A good fire burned in a small old-fashioned grate, but there was no other light. The inn was closed to customers, it being past eleven o'clock. On a bare table I perceived a candle, and ventured to put a match to it. I then saw almost exactly such a room as one would expect to find at the rear of the bar-parlour of an inn on the outskirts of an industrial town. It

46

appeared to serve the double purpose of a living-room and of a retreat for favoured customers. The table was evidently one at which men drank. On a shelf was a row of bottles, more or less empty, bearing names famous in newspaper advertisements and in the House of Lords. The dozen chairs suggested an acute bodily discomfort such as would only be tolerated by a sitter all of whose sensory faculties were centred in his palate. On a broken chair in a corner was an insecure pile of books. A smaller table was covered with a chequered cloth on which were a few plates. Along one wall, under the window, ran a pitch-pine sofa upholstered with a stuff slightly dissimilar from that on the table. The mattress of the sofa was uneven and its surface wrinkled, and old newspapers and pieces of brown paper had been stowed away between it and the framework. The chief article of furniture was an effective walnut bookcase, the glass doors of which were curtained with red cloth. The window, wider than it was high, was also curtained with red cloth. The walls, papered in a saffron tint, bore framed advertisements and a few photographs of self-conscious persons. The ceiling was as obscure as heaven; the floor tiled, with a list rug in front of the steel fender.

I put my overcoat on the sofa, picked up the candle and glanced at the books in the corner: Lavater's indestructible work, a paper-covered Whitaker, the Licensed Victuallers' Almanac, Johnny Ludlow, the illustrated catalogue of the Exhibition of 1856, Cruden's Concordance, and seven or eight volumes of Knight's Penny Encyclopaedia. While I was poring on these titles I heard movements overhead - previously there had been no sound whatever - and with guilty haste I restored the candle to the table and placed myself negligently in front of the fire.

"Now don't let me see ye up here any more till I fetch ye!" said a woman's distant voice, not crossly, but firmly. And then, crossly: "Be off with ye now!"

Reluctant boots on the stairs! Jos Myatt entered to me. He did not speak at first; nor did I. He avoided my glance. He was still wearing the cut-away coat with the line of mud up the back. I took out my watch, not for the sake of information, but from mere nervousness, and the sight of the watch reminded me that it would be prudent to wind it up.

"Better not forget that," I said, winding it.

"Ay!" said he, gloomily. "It's a tip." And he wound up his watch; a large, thick, golden one.

This watch-winding established a basis of intercourse between us.

"I hope everything is going on all right," I murmured.

"What dun ye say?" he asked.

"I say I hope everything is going on all right," I repeated louder, and jerked my head in the direction of the stairs, to indicate the place from which he had come.

"Oh!" he exclaimed, as if surprised. "Now what'll ye have, mester?" He stood waiting. "It's my call to-night."

I explained to him that I never took alcohol. It was not quite true, but it was as true as most general propositions are.

"Neither me!" he said shortly, after a pause.

"You're a teetotaller too?" I showed a little involuntary astonishment.

He put forward his chin.

"What do you think?" he said confidentially and scornfully. It was precisely as if he had said: "Do you think that anybody but a born ass would not be a teetotaller, in my position?"

I sat down on a chair.

"Take th' squab, mester," he said, pointing to the sofa. I took it.

He picked up the candle; then dropped it, and lighted a lamp which was on the mantelpiece between his vases of blue glass. His movements were very slow, hesitating and clumsy. Blowing out the candle, which smoked for a long time, he went with the lamp to the bookcase. As the key of the bookcase was in his right pocket and the lamp in his right hand he had to change the lamp, cautiously, from hand to hand. When he opened the cupboard I saw a rich gleam of silver from every shelf of it except the lowest, and I could distinguish the forms of ceremonial cups with pedestals and immense handles.

"I suppose these are your pots?" I said.

"Ay!"
He displayed to me the fruits of his manifold victories. I could see him straining along endless cinder-paths and highroads under hot suns, his great knees going up and down like treadles amid the plaudits and howls of vast populations. And all that now remained of that glory was these debased and vicious shapes, magnificently useless, grossly ugly, with their inscriptions lost in a mess of flourishes.

"Ay!" he said again, when I had fingered the last of them.

"A very fine show indeed!" I said, resuming the sofa.

He took a penny bottle of ink and a pen out of the bookcase, and also, from the lowest shelf, a bag of money and a long narrow account book. Then he sat down at the table and commenced accountancy. It was clear that he regarded his task as formidable and complex. To see him reckoning the coins, manipulating the pen, splashing the ink, scratching the page; to hear him whispering consecutive numbers aloud, and muttering mysterious anathemas against the untamable naughtiness of figures, all this was painful, and with the painfulness of a simple exercise rendered difficult by inaptitude and incompetence. I wanted to jump up and cry to him: "Get out of the way, man, and let me do it for you! I can do it while you are wiping hairs from your pen on your sleeve." I was sorry for him because he was ridiculous and even more grotesque than ridiculous. I felt, quite acutely, that it was a shame that he could not be forever the central figure of a field of mud, kicking a ball into long and grandiose parabolas higher than gasometers, or breaking an occasional leg, surrounded by the violent affection of hearts whose melting-point was the exclamation, "Good old Jos!" I felt that if he must repose his existence ought to have been so contrived that he could repose in impassive and senseless dignity, like a mountain watching the flight of time. The conception of him tracing symbols in a ledger, counting shillings and sixpences, descending to arithmetic, and suffering those humiliations which are the invariable preliminaries to legitimate fatherhood, was shocking to a nice taste for harmonious fitness.... What, this precious and terrific organism, this slave with a specialty--whom distant towns had once been anxious to buy at the prodigious figure of five hundred pounds--obliged to sit in a mean chamber and wait silently while the woman of his choice encountered the supreme peril! And he would "soon be past football!" He was "thirty-four if a day!"

It was the verge of senility! He was no longer worth five hundred pounds. Perhaps even now this jointed merchandise was only worth two hundred pounds! And "they" the shadowy directors, who could not kick a ball fifty feet and who would probably turn sick if they broke a leg "they" paid him four pounds a week for being the hero of a quarter of a million of people! He was the chief magnet to draw fifteen thousand sixpences and shillings of a Saturday afternoon into a company's cash box, and here he sat splitting his head over fewer sixpences and shillings than would fill a half-pint pot! Jos, you ought in justice to have been Jose, with a thin red necktie down your breast (instead of a line of mud up your back), and embroidered breeches on those miraculous legs, and an income of a quarter of a million pesetas, and the languishing acquiescence of innumerable mantillas. Every moment you were getting older and stiffer; every moment was bringing nearer the moment when young men would reply curtly to their doddering elders: "Jos Myatt - who was 'e?"

The putting away of the ledger, the ink, the pen and the money was as exasperating as their taking out had been. Then Jos, always too large for the room, crossed the tiled floor and mended the fire. A poker was more suited to his capacity than a pen. He glanced about him, uncertain and anxious, and then crept to the door near the foot of the stairs and listened. There was no sound; and that was curious. The woman who was bringing into the world the hero's child made no cry that reached us below. Once or twice I had heard muffled movements not quite overhead somewhere above but naught else. The doctor and Jos's sister seemed to have retired into a sinister and dangerous mystery. I could not dispel from my mind pictures of what they were watching and what they were doing.

The vast, cruel, fumbling clumsiness of Nature, her lack of majesty in crises that ought to be majestic, her incurable indignity, disgusted me, aroused my disdain, I wanted, as a philosopher of all the cultures, to feel that the present was indeed a majestic crisis, to be so esteemed by a superior man. I could not. Though the crisis possibly intimidated me somewhat, yet, on behalf of Jos Myatt, I was ashamed of it. This may be reprehensible, but it is true.

He sat down by the fire and looked at the fire. I could not attempt to carry on a conversation with him, and to avoid the necessity for any talk at all, I extended myself on the sofa and averted my face, wondering once again why I had accompanied the doctor to Toft End. The doctor was now in another, an inaccessible world. I dozed, and from my doze I was roused by Jos Myatt going to the door on the stairs.

"Jos," said a voice. "It's a girl."

Then a silence.

I admit there was a flutter in my heart. Another soul, another formed and unchangeable temperament, tumbled into the world! Whence? Whither?... As for the quality of majesty, yes, if silver trumpets had announced the advent, instead of a stout, aproned woman, the moment could not have been more majestic in its sadness. I say "sadness," which is the inevitable and sole effect of these eternal and banal questions, "Whence? Whither?"

"Is her bad?" Jos whispered.

"Her's pretty bad," said the voice, but cheerily. "Bring me up another scuttle o' coal."

When he returned to the parlour, after being again dismissed, I said to him:

"Well, I congratulate you."

"I thank ye!" he said, and sat down. Presently I could hear him muttering to himself, mildly: "Hell! Hell! Hell!"

I thought: "Stirling will not be very long now, and we can depart home." I looked at my watch. It was a quarter to two. But Stirling did not appear, nor was there any message from him or sign. I had to submit to the predicament. As a faint chilliness from the window affected my back I drew my overcoat up to my shoulders as a counterpane. Through a gap between the red curtains of the window I could see a star blazing. It passed behind the curtain with disconcerting rapidity. The universe was swinging and whirling as usual.

VII

Sounds of knocking disturbed me. In the few seconds that elapsed before I could realize just where I was and why I was there, the summoning knocks were repeated. The early sun was shining through the red blind. I sat up and straightened my hair, involuntarily composing my attitude so that nobody who might enter the room should imagine that I had been other than patiently wide-awake all night. The second door of the parlour, that leading to the bar-room of the Foaming Quart was open, and I could see the bar itself, with shelves rising behind it and the upright handles of a beer-engine at one end. Someone whom I could not see was evidently unbolting and unlocking the principal entrance to the inn. Then I heard the scraping of a creaky portal on the floor.

"Well, Jos lad!"

It was the voice of the little man, Charlie, who had spoken with Myatt on the football field.

"Come in quick, Charlie. It's cowd [cold]," said the voice of Jos Myatt, gloomily.

"Ay! Cowd it is, lad! It's above three mile as I've walked, and thou knows it, Jos. Give us a quartern o' gin."

The door grated again and a bolt was drawn.

The two men passed together behind the bar, and so within my vision. Charlie had a grey muffler round his neck; his hands were far in his pockets and seemed to be at strain, as though trying to prevent his upper and his lower garments from flying apart. Jos Myatt was extremely dishevelled. In the little man's demeanour towards the big one there was now none of the self-conscious pride in the mere fact of acquaintance that I had noticed on the field. Clearly the two were intimate friends, perhaps relatives. While Jos was dispensing the gin, Charlie said, in a low tone:

"Well, what luck, Jos?"

This was the first reference, by either of them, to the crisis.

Jos deliberately finished pouring out the gin. Then he said:

"There's two on 'em, Charlie."

"Two on 'em? What mean'st tha', lad?"

"I mean as it's twins."

Charlie and I were equally startled.

"Thou never says!" he murmured, incredulous.

"Ay! One o' both sorts," said Jos.

"Thou never says!" Charlie repeated, holding his glass of gin steady in his hand.

"One come at summat after one o'clock, and th' other between five and six. I had for fetch old woman Eardley to help. It were more than a handful for Susannah and th' doctor."

Astonishing, that I should have slept through these events!

"How is her?" asked Charlie, quietly, as it were casually. I think this appearance of casualness was caused by the stoic suppression of the symptoms of anxiety.

"Her's bad," said Jos, briefly.

"And I am na' surprised," said Charlie. And he lifted the glass. "Well, here's luck." He sipped the gin, savouring it on his tongue like a connoisseur, and gradually making up his mind about its quality. Then he took another sip.

"Hast seen her?"

"I seed her for a minute, but our Susannah wouldna' let me stop i' th' room. Her was raving like."

"Missis?"

"Ay!"

"And th' babbies, hast seen them?"

"Ay! But I can make nowt out of 'em. Mrs Eardley says as her's never seen no finer."

"Doctor gone?"

"That he has na'! He's bin up there all the blessed night, in his shirt-sleeves. I give him a stiff glass o' whisky at five o'clock and that's all as he's had."

Charlie finished his gin. The pair stood silent.

"Well," said Charlie, striking his leg. "Swelp me bob! It fair beats me! Twins! Who'd ha'thought it? Jos, lad, thou mayst be thankful as it isna' triplets. Never did I think, as I was footing it up here this morning, as it was twins I was coming to!"

"Hast got that half quid in thy pocket?"

"What half quid?" said Charlie, defensively.

"Now then. Chuck us it over!" said Jos, suddenly harsh and overbearing.

"I laid thee half quid as it 'ud be a wench," said Charlie, doggedly.

"Thou'rt a liar, Charlie!" said Jos. "Thou laidst half a quid as it wasna' a boy."

"Nay, nay!" Charlie shook his head.

"And a boy it is!" Jos persisted.

"It being a lad and a wench," said Charlie, with a judicial air, "and me 'aving laid as it 'ud be a wench, I wins." In his accents and his gestures I could discern the mean soul, who on principle never paid until he was absolutely forced to pay. I could see also that Jos Myatt knew his man.

"Thou laidst me as it wasna' a lad," Jos almost shouted. "And a lad it is, I tell thee."

"And a wench!" said Charlie; then shook his head.

The wrangle proceeded monotonously, each party repeating over and over again the phrases of his own argument. I was very glad that Jos did not know me to be a witness of the making of the bet; otherwise I should assuredly have been summoned to give judgment.

"Let's call it off, then," Charlie suggested at length. "That'll settle it. And it being twins"

"Nay, thou old devil, I'll none call it off. Thou owes me half a quid, and I'll have it out of thee."

"Look ye here," Charlie said more softly. "I'll tell thee what'll settle it. Which on 'em come first, th' lad or th'wench?"

"Th' wench come first," Jos Myatt admitted, with resentful reluctance, dully aware that defeat was awaiting him.

"Well, then! Th' wench is thy eldest child. That's law, that is. And what was us betting about, Jos lad? Us was betting about thy eldest and no other. I'll admit as I laid it wasna' a lad, as thou sayst. And it wasna' a lad. First come is eldest, and us was betting about eldest."

Charlie stared at the father in triumph.

Jos Myatt pushed roughly past him in the narrow space behind the bar, and came into the parlour. Nodding to me curtly, he unlocked the bookcase and took two crown pieces from a leathern purse which lay next to the bag. Then he returned to the bar and banged the coins on the counter with fury.

"Take thy brass!" he shouted angrily. "Take thy brass! But thou'rt a damned shark, Charlie, and if anybody 'ud give me a plug o' bacca for doing it, I'd bash thy face in."

The other sniggered contentedly as he picked up his money.

"A bet's a bet," said Charlie.

He was clearly accustomed to an occasional violence of demeanour from Jos Myatt, and felt no fear. But he was wrong in feeling no fear. He had not allowed, in his estimate of the situation, for the exasperated condition of Jos Hyatt's nerves under the unique experiences of the night.

Jos's face twisted into a hundred wrinkles and his hand seized Charlie by the arm whose hand held the coins.

"Drop 'em!" he cried loudly, repenting his naive honesty. "Drop 'em! Or I'll"

The stout woman, her apron all soiled, now came swiftly and scarce heard into the parlour, and stood at the door leading to the bar-room.

"What's up, Susannah?" Jos demanded in a new voice.

"Well may ye ask what's up!" said the woman. "Shouting and brangling there, ye sots!"

"What's up?" Jos demanded again, loosing Charlie's arm.

"Her's gone!" the woman feebly whimpered. "Like that!" with a vague movement of the hand indicating suddenness. Then she burst into wild sobs and rushed madly back whence she had come, and the sound of her sobs diminished as she ascended the stairs, and expired altogether in the distant shutting of a door.

The men looked at each other.

Charlie restored the crown-pieces to the counter and pushed them towards Jos.

"Here!" he murmured faintly.

Jos flung them savagely to the ground. Another pause followed.

"As God is my witness," he exclaimed solemnly, his voice saturated with feeling, "as God is my witness," he repeated, "I'll ne'er touch a footba' again!"

Little Charlie gazed up at him sadly, plaintively, for what seemed a long while.

"It's good-bye to th' First League, then, for Knype!" he tragically muttered, at length.

VIII

Dr Stirling drove the car very slowly back to Bursley. We glided gently down into the populous valleys. All the stunted trees were coated with rime, which made the sharpest contrast with their black branches and the black mud under us. The high chimneys sent forth their black smoke calmly and tirelessly into the fresh blue sky. Sunday had descended on the vast landscape like a physical influence. We saw a snake of children winding out of a dark brown Sunday school into a dark brown chapel. And up from the valleys came all the bells of all the temples of all the different gods of the Five Towns, chiming, clanging, ringing, each insisting that it alone invited to the altar of the one God. And priests and acolytes of the various cults hurried occasionally along, in silk hats and bright neckties, and smooth coats with folded handkerchiefs sticking out of the pockets, busy, happy and self-important, the convinced heralds of eternal salvation: no doubt nor hesitation as to any fundamental truth had ever entered their minds. We passed through a long, straight street of new red houses with blue slate roofs, all gated and gardened. Here and there a girl with her hair in pins and a rough brown apron over a gaudy frock was stoning a front step. And half-way down the street a man in a scarlet jersey, supported by two women in blue bonnets, was beating a drum and crying aloud: "My friends, you may die to-night. Where, I ask you, where?" But he had no friends; not even a boy heeded him. The drum continued to bang in our rear.

I enjoyed all this. All this seemed to me to be fine, seemed to throw off the true, fine, romantic savour of life. I would have altered nothing in it. Mean, harsh, ugly, squalid, crude, barbaric--yes, but what an intoxicating sense in it of the organized vitality of a vast community unconscious of itself! I would have altered nothing even in the events of the night. I thought of the rooms at the top of the staircase of the Foaming Quart, mysterious rooms which I had not seen and never should see, recondite rooms from which a soul had slipped away and into which two had come, scenes of anguish and of frustrated effort! Historical rooms, surely! And yet not a house in the hundreds of houses past which we slid but possessed rooms ennobled and made august by happenings exactly as impressive in their tremendous inexplicableness.

The natural humanity of Jos Myatt and Charlie, their fashion of comporting themselves in a sudden stress, pleased me. How else should they have behaved? I could understand Charlie's prophetic dirge over the ruin of the Knype Football Club. It was not that he did not feel the tragedy in the house. He had felt it, and because he had felt it he had uttered at random, foolishly, the first clear thought that ran into his head.

Stirling was quiet. He appeared to be absorbed in steering, and looked straight in front, yawning now and again. He was much more fatigued than I was. Indeed, I had slept pretty well. He said, as we swerved into Trafalgar Road and overtook the aristocracy on its way to chapel and church: "Well, ye let yeself in for a night, young man! No mistake!"

He smiled, and I smiled.

"What's going to occur up there?" I asked, indicating Toft End.

"What do you mean?"

"A man like that left with two babies!"

"Oh!" he said. "They'll manage that all right. His sister's a widow. She'll go and live with him. She's as fond of those infants already as if they were her own."

We drew up at his double gates.

"Be sure ye explain to Brindley," he said, as I left him, "that it isn't my fault ye've had a night out of bed. It was your own doing. I'm going to get a bit of sleep now. See you this evening, Bob's asked me to supper."

A servant was sweeping Bob Brindley's porch and the front door was open. I went in. The sound of the piano guided me to the drawing-room. Brindley, the morning cigarette between his lips, was playing one of Maurice Ravel's "L'heure espagnole." He held his head back so as to keep the smoke out of his eyes. His children in their blue jerseys were building bricks on the carpet.

Without ceasing to play he addressed me calmly:

"You're a nice chap! Where the devil have you been?"

And one of the little boys, glancing up, said, with roguish, imitative innocence, in his high, shrill voice:

"Where the del you been?"

The Letter And The Lie By Arnold Bennett

I

As he hurried from his brougham through the sombre hall to his study, leaving his secretary far in the rear, he had already composed the first sentence of his address to the United Chambers of Commerce of the Five Towns; his mind was full of it; he sat down at once to his vast desk, impatient to begin dictating. Then it was that he perceived the letter, lodged prominently against the gold and onyx inkstand given to him on his marriage by the Prince and Princess of Wales. The envelope was imperfectly fastened, or not fastened at all, and the flap came apart as he fingered it nervously.

"Dear Cloud,--This is to say good-bye, finally"

He stopped. Fear took him at the heart, as though he had been suddenly told by a physician that he must submit to an operation endangering his life. And he skipped feverishly over the four pages to the signature, "Yours sincerely, Gertrude."

The secretary entered.

"I must write one or two private letters first," he said to the secretary. "Leave me. I'll ring."

"Yes, sir. Shall I take your overcoat?"

"No, no."

A discreet closing of the door.

"-finally. I can't stand it any longer. Cloud, I'm gone to Italy. I shall use the villa at Florence, and trust you to leave me alone. You must tell our friends. You can start with the Bargraves tonight. I'm sure they'll agree with me it's for the best"

It seemed to him that this letter was very like the sort of letter that gets read in the Divorce Court and printed in the papers afterwards; and he felt sick.

"-for the best. Everybody will know in a day or two, and then in another day or two the affair will be forgotten. It's difficult to write naturally under the circumstances, so all I'll say is that we aren't suited to each other, Cloud. Ten years of marriage has amply proved that, though I knew it six— seven years ago. You haven't guessed that you've been killing me all these years; but it is so"

Killing her! He flushed with anger, with indignation, with innocence, with guilt with Heaven knew what!

"- it is so. You've been living your life. But what about me? In five more years I shall be old, and I haven't begun to live. I can't stand it any longer. I can't stand this awful Five Towns district"

Had he not urged her many a time to run up to South Audley Street for a change, and leave him to continue his work? Nobody wanted her to be always in Staffordshire!

"-and I can't stand you. That's the brutal truth. You've got on my nerves, my poor boy, with your hurry, and your philanthropy, and your commerce, and your seriousness. My poor nerves! And you've been too busy to notice it. You fancied I should be content if you made love to me absent-mindedly, en passant, between a political dinner and a bishop's breakfast."

He flinched. She had stung him.

"I sting you"

No! And he straightened himself, biting his lips!

"-I sting you! I'm rude! I'm inexcusable! People don't say these things, not even hysterical wives to impeccable husbands, eh? I admit it. But I was bound to tell you. You're a serious person, Cloud, and I'm not. Still, we were both born as we are, and I've just as much right to be unserious as you have to be serious. That's what you've never realized. You aren't better than me; you're only different from me. It is unfortunate that there are some aspects of the truth that you are incapable of grasping. However, after this morning's scene--"

Scene? What scene? He remembered no scene, except that he had asked her not to interrupt him while he was reading his letters, had asked her quite politely, and she had left the breakfast-table. He thought she had left because she had finished. He hadn't a notion, what nonsense!

"- this morning's scene, I decided not to 'interrupt' you anymore"

Yes. There was the word he had used; how childish she was!

"- any more in the contemplation of those aspects of the truth which you are capable of grasping. Good-bye! You're an honest man, and a straight man, and very conscientious, and very clever, and I expect you're doing a lot of good in the world. But your responsibilities are too much for you. I relieve you of one, quite minor one; your wife. You don't want a wife. What you want is a doll that you can wind up once a fortnight to say 'Good-morning, dear,' and 'Good-night, dear.' I think I can manage without a husband for a very long time. I'm not so bitter as you might guess from this letter, Cloud. But I want you thoroughly to comprehend that it's finished between us. You can do what you like. People can say what they like. I've had enough. I'll pay any price for freedom. Good luck. Best wishes. I would write this letter afresh if I thought I could do a better one. Yours sincerely, Gertrude."

He dropped the letter, picked it up and read it again and then folded it in his accustomed tidy manner and replaced it in the envelope. He sat down and propped the letter against the inkstand and stared at the address in her careless hand: "The Right Honourable Sir Cloud Malpas, Baronet." She had written the address in full like that as a last stroke of sarcasm. And she had not even put "Private."

He was dizzy, nearly stunned; his head rang.

Then he rose and went to the window. The high hill on which stood Malpas Manor, the famous Rat Edge, fell away gradually to the south, and in the distance below him, miles off, the black smoke of the Five Towns loomed above the yellow fires of blast-furnaces. He was the demi-god of the district, a greater landowner than even the Earl of Chell, a model landlord, a model employer of four thousand men, a model proprietor of seven pits and two iron foundries, a philanthropist, a religionist, the ornamental mayor of Knype, chairman of a Board of Guardians, governor of hospitals, president of Football Association, in short, Sir Cloud, son of Sir Cloud and grandson of Sir Cloud.

He stared dreamily at his dominion. Scandal, then, was to touch him with her smirching finger, him the spotless! Gertrude had fled. He had ruined Gertrude's life! Had he? With his heavy and severe conscientiousness he asked himself whether he was to blame in her regard. Yes, he thought he was to blame. It stood to reason that he was to blame. Women, especially such as Gertrude, proud, passionate, reserved, don't do these things for nothing.

With a sigh he passed into his dressing-room and dropped on to a sofa.

She would be inflexible he knew her. His mind dwelt on the beautiful first days of their marriage, the tenderness and the dream! And now!

He heard footsteps in the study; the door was opened! It was Gertrude! He could see her in the dusk. She had returned! Why? She tripped to the desk, leaned forward and snatched at the letter. Evidently she did not know that he was in the house and had read it.

The tension was too painful. A sigh broke from him, as it were of physical torture.

"Who's there?" she cried, in a startled voice. "Is that you, Cloud?"

"Yes," he breathed.

"But you're home very early!" Her voice shook.

"I'm not well, Gertrude," he replied. "I'm tired. I came in here to lie down. Can't you do something for my head? I must have a holiday."

He heard her crunch up the letter, and then she hastened to him in the dressing-room.

"My poor Cloud!" she said, bending over him in the mature elegance of her thirty years. He noticed her travelling costume. "Some eau de Cologne?"

He nodded weakly.

"We'll go away for a holiday," he said, later, as she bathed his forehead.

The touch of her hands on his temples reminded him of forgotten caresses. And he did really feel as though, within a quarter of an hour, he had been through a long and dreadful illness and was now convalescent.

II

"Then you think that after starting she thought better of it?" said Lord Bargrave after dinner that night. "And came back?"

Lord Bargrave was Gertrude's cousin, and he and his wife sometimes came over from Shropshire for a week-end. He sat with Sir Cloud in the smoking-room; a man with greying hair and a youngish, equable face.

"Yes, Harry, that was it. You see, I'd just happened to put the letter exactly where I found it. She's no notion that I've seen it."

"She's a thundering good actress!" observed Lord Bargrave, sipping some whisky. "I knew something was up at dinner, but I didn't know it from her: I knew it from you."

Sir Cloud smiled sadly.

"Well, you see, I'm supposed to be ill at least, to be not well."

"You'd best take her away at once," said Lord Bargrave. "And don't do it clumsily. Say you'll go away for a few days, and then gradually lengthen it out. She mentioned Italy, you say. Well, let it be Italy. Clear out for six months."

"But my work here?"

"D--n your work here!" said Lord Bargrave. "Do you suppose you're indispensable here? Do you suppose the Five Towns can't manage without you? Our caste is decayed, my boy, and silly fools like you try to lengthen out the miserable last days of its importance by giving yourselves airs in industrial districts!
Your conscience tells you that what the demagogues say is true we are rotters on the face of the earth, we are mediaeval; and you try to drown your conscience in the noise of philanthropic speeches. There isn't a sensible working-man in the Five Towns who doesn't, at the bottom of his heart, assess you at your true value as nothing but a man with a hobby, and plenty of time and money to ride it."

"I do not agree with you," Sir Cloud said stiffly.

"Yes, you do," said Lord Bargrave. "At the same time I admire you, Cloud. I'm not built the same way myself, but I admire you except in the matter of Gertrude. There you've been wrong, of course from the highest motives: which makes it all the worse. A man oughtn't to put hobbies above the wife of his bosom. And, besides, she's one of us. So take her away and stay away and make love to her."

"Suppose I do? Suppose I try? I must tell her!"

"Tell her what?"

"That I read the letter. I acted a lie to her this afternoon. I can't let that lie stand between us. It would not be right."

Lord Bargrave sprang up.

"Cloud," he cried. "For heaven's sake, don't be an infernal ass. Here you've escaped a domestic catastrophe of the first magnitude by a miracle. You've made a sort of peace with Gertrude. She's come to her senses. And now you want to mess up the whole show by the act of an idiot! What if you did act a lie to her this afternoon? A very good thing! The most sensible thing you've done for years! Let the lie stand between you. Look at it carefully every morning when you awake. It will help you to avoid repeating in the future the high-minded errors of the past. See?"

III

And in Lady Bargrave's dressing-room that night Gertrude was confiding in Lady Bargrave.

"Yes," she said, "Cloud must have come in within five minutes of my leaving--two hours earlier than he was expected. Fortunately he went straight to his dressing-room. Or was it unfortunately? I was half-way to the station when it occurred to me that I hadn't fastened the envelope! You see, I was naturally in an awfully nervous state, Minnie. So I told Collins to turn back. Fuge, our new butler, is of an extremely curious disposition, and I couldn't bear the idea of him prying about and perhaps reading that letter before Cloud got it. And just as I was picking up the letter to fasten it I heard Cloud in the next room. Oh! I never felt so queer in all my life! The poor boy was quite unwell. I screwed up the letter and went to him. What else could I do? And really he was so tired and white well, it moved me! It moved me. And when he spoke about going away I suddenly thought: 'Why not try to make a new start with him?' After all ..."

There was a pause.

"What did you say in the letter?" Lady Bargrave demanded. "How did you put it?"

"I'll read it to you," said Gertrude, and she took the letter from her corsage and began to read it. She got as far as "I can't stand this awful Five Towns district," and then she stopped.
"Well, go on," Lady Bargrave encouraged her.

"No," said Gertrude, and she put the letter in the fire. "The fact is," she said, going to Lady Bargrave's chair, "it was too cruel. I hadn't realized.... I must have been very worked-up.... One does work oneself up.... Things seem a little different now...." She glanced at her companion.

"Why, Gertrude, you're crying, dearest!"

"What a chance it was!" murmured Gertrude, in her tears. "What a chance! Because, you know, if he had once read it I would never have gone back on it. I'm that sort of woman. But as it is, there's a sort of hope of a sort of happiness, isn't there?"

"Gertrude!" It was Sir Cloud's voice, gentle and tender, outside the door.

"Mercy on us!" exclaimed Lady Bargrave. "It's half-past one. Bargrave will have been asleep long since."

Gertrude kissed her in silence, opened the door, and left her.

A Feud By Arnold Bennett

When Clive Timmis paused at the side-door of Ezra Brunt's great shop in Machin Street, and the door was opened to him by Ezra Brunt's daughter before he had had time to pull the bell, not only all Machin Street knew it within the hour, but also most persons of consequence left in Hanbridge on a Thursday afternoon; Thursday being early-closing day. For Hanbridge, though it counts sixty thousand inhabitants, and is the chief of the Five Towns, that vast, huddled congeries of boroughs devoted to the manufacture of earthenware, is a place where the art of attending to other people's business still flourishes in rustic perfection.

Ezra Brunt's drapery establishment was the foremost retail house, in any branch of trade, of the Five Towns. It had no rival nearer than Manchester, thirty-six miles off; and even Manchester could exhibit nothing conspicuously superior to it. The most acutely critical shoppers of the Five Towns women who were in the habit of going to London every year for the January sales spoke of Brunt's as a 'right-down good shop.' And the husbands of these ladies, manufacturers who employed from two hundred to a thousand men, regarded Ezra Brunt as a commercial magnate of equal importance with themselves. Brunt, who had served his apprenticeship at Birmingham, started business in Machin Street in 1862, when Hanbridge was half its present size and all the best shops of the district were in Oldcastle, an ancient burg contiguous with, but holding itself proudly aloof from, the industrial Five Towns. He paid eighty pour ds a year rent, and lived over the shop, and in the summer quarter his gas bill was always under a sovereign. For ten years success tarried, but in 1872 his daughter Eva was born and his wife died, and from that moment the sun of his prosperity climbed higher and higher into heaven. He had been profoundly attached to his wife, and, having lost her he abandoned himself to the mercantile struggle with that morose and terrible ferocity which was the root of his character. Of rude, gaunt aspect, gruffly taciturn by nature, and variable in temper, he yet had the precious instinct for soothing customers. To this day he can surpass his own shop-walkers in the admirable and tender solicitude with which, forsaking dialect, he drops into a lady's ear his famous stereotyped phrase: 'Are you receiving proper attention, madam?' From the first he eschewed the facile trickeries and ostentations which allure the populace. He sought a high-class trade, and by waiting he found it.

He would never advertise on hoardings; for many years he had no signboard over his shop-front; and whereas the name of 'Bostocks,' the huge cheap drapers lower down Machin Street, on the opposite side, attacks you at every railway-station and in every tramcar, the name of 'E. Brunt' is to be seen only in a modest regular advertisement on the front page of the Staffordshire Signal. Repose, reticence, respectability--it was these attributes which he decided his shop should possess, and by means of which he succeeded. To enter Brunt's, with its silently swinging doors, its broad, easy staircases, its long floors covered with warm, red linoleum, its partitioned walls, its smooth mahogany counters, its unobtrusive mirrors, its rows of youths and virgins in black, and its pervading atmosphere of quietude and discretion, was like entering a temple before the act of oblation has commenced. You were conscious of some supreme administrative influence everywhere imposing itself. That influence was Ezra Brunt. And yet the man differed utterly from the thing he had created. His was one of those dark and passionate souls which smoulder in this harsh Midland district as slag-heaps smoulder on the pit-banks, revealing their strange fires only in the darkness.

In 1899 Brunt's establishment occupied four shops, Nos. 52, 56, 58, and 60, in Machin Street. He had bought the freeholds at a price which timid people regarded as exorbitant, but the solicitors of Hanbridge secretly applauded his enterprise and shrewdness in anticipating the enormous rise in ground-values which has now been in rapid, steady progress there for more than a decade. He had thrown the interiors together and rebuilt the frontages in handsome freestone. He had also purchased several shops opposite, and rumour said that it was his intention to offer these latter to the Town Council at a low figure if the Council would cut a new street leading from his premises to the Market Square. Such a scheme would have met with general approval. But there was one serious hiatus in the plans of Ezra Brunt to wit, No. 54, Machin Street. No. 54, separating 52 and 56, was a chemist's shop, shabby but sedate as to appearance, owned and occupied by George Christopher Timmis, a mild and venerable citizen, and a local preacher in the Wesleyan Methodist Connexion. For nearly thirty years Brunt had coveted Mr. Timmis's shop; more than twenty years have elapsed since he first opened negotiations for it. Mr. Timmis was by no means eager to sell--indeed, his attitude was distinctly a repellent one--but a bargain would undoubtedly have been concluded had not a report reached the ears of Mr. Timmis to the effect that Ezra Brunt had remarked at the Turk's Head that 'th' old leech was only sticking out for every brass farthing he could get.' The report was untrue, but Mr. Timmis believed it, and from that moment Ezra Brunt's chances of obtaining the chemist's shop vanished completely. His lawyer expended diplomacy in vain, raising the offer week by week till the incredible sum of three thousand pounds was reached. Then Ezra Brunt himself saw Mr. Timmis, and without a word of prelude said:

'Will ye take three thousand guineas for this bit o' property?'

'Not thirty thousand guineas,' said Mr. Timmis quietly; the stern pride of the benevolent old local preacher had been aroused.

'Then be damned to you!' said Ezra Brunt, who had never been known to swear before.

Thenceforth a feud existed, not less bitter because it was a feud in which nothing was said and nothing done a silent and implacable mutual resistance. The sole outward sign of it was the dirty and stumpy brown-brick shop-front of Mr. Timmis, squeezed in between those massive luxurious facades of stone which Ezra Brunt soon afterwards erected. The pharmaceutical business of Mr. Timmis was not a very large one, and, fiscally, Ezra Brunt could have swallowed him at a meal and suffered no inconvenience; but in that the aged chemist had lived on just half his small income for some fifty years past, his position was impregnable. Hanbridge smiled cynically at this impasse produced by an idle word, and, recognising the equality of the antagonists, leaned neither to one side nor to the other.

At intervals, however, the legend of the feud was embroidered with new and effective detail in the mouth of some inventive gossip, and by degrees it took high place among those piquant social histories which illustrate the real life of a town, and which parents recount to their children with such zest in moods of reminiscence.

When George Christopher Timmis buried his wife, Ezra Brunt, as a near neighbour, was asked to the funeral. 'The cortege will move at 1.30,' ran the printed invitation, and at 1.15 Brunt's carriage was decorously in place behind the hearse and the two mourning-coaches. The demeanour of the chemist and the draper towards each other was a sublime answer to the demands of the occasion; some people even said that the breach had been healed, but these were not of the discerning.

The most active person at the funeral was the chemist's only nephew, Clive Timmis, partner in a small but prosperous firm of majolica manufacturers at Bursley. Clive, who was seldom seen in Hanbridge, made a favourable impression on everyone by his pleasing, unaffected manner and his air of discretion and success. He was a bachelor of thirty-two, and lived in lodgings at Bursley. On the return of the funeral-party from the cemetery, Clive Timmis found Brunt's daughter Eva in his uncle's house. Uninvited, she had left her place in the private room at her father's shop in order to assist Timmis's servant Sarah in the preparation of that solid and solemn repast which must inevitably follow every proper interment in the Five Towns. Without false modesty, she introduced herself to one or two of the men who had surprised her at her work, and then quietly departed just as they were sitting down to table and Sarah had brought in the hot tea-cakes. Clive Timmis saw her only for a moment, but from that moment she was his one thought. During the evening, which he spent alone with his uncle, he behaved in every particular as a nephew should, yet he was acting a part; his real self roved after Ezra Brunt's daughter, wherever she might be. Clive had never fallen in love, though several times in his life he had tried hard to do so. He had long wished to marry wished ardently; he had even got into the way of regarding every woman he met and he met many in the light of a possible partner. 'Can it be she? he had asked himself a thousand times, and then answered half sadly, 'No.' Not one woman had touched his imagination, coincided with his dream. It is strange that after seeing Eva Brunt he forgot thus to interrogate himself. For a fortnight, while he went his ways as usual, her image occupied his heart, throwing that once orderly chamber into the wildest confusion; and he let it remain, dimly aware of some delicious danger. He inspected the image every night before he slept, and every morning when he awoke, and made no effort to define its distracting charm; he knew only that Eva Brunt was absolutely and in every detail unlike all other women. On the second Sunday he murmured during the sermon: 'But I only saw her for a minute.' A few days afterwards he took the tram to Hanbridge.

'Uncle,' he said, 'how should you like me to come and live here with you? I've been thinking things out a bit, and I thought perhaps you'd like it. I expect you must feel rather lonely now.'

The neat, fragrant shop was empty, and the two men stood behind the big glass-fronted case of Burroughs and Wellcome's preparations. Clive's venerable uncle happened to be looking into a drawer marked 'Gentianae Rad. Pulv.' He closed the drawer with slow hesitation, and then, stroking his long white beard, replied in that deliberate voice which seemed always to tremble with religious fervour:

'The hand of the Lord is in this thing, Clive. I have wished that you might come to live here with me. But I was afraid it would be too far from the works.'

'Pooh! that's nothing,' said Clive.

As he lingered at the shop door for the Bursley car to pass the end of Machin Street, Eva Brunt went by. He raised his hat with diffidence, and she smiled. It was a marvellous chance. His heart leapt into a throb which was half agony and half delight.

'I am in love,' he said gravely.

He had just discovered the fact, and the discovery filled him with exquisite apprehension.

If he had waited till the age of thirty-two for that springtime of the soul which we call love, Clive had not waited for nothing. Eva was a woman to enravish the heart of a man whose imagination could pierce the agitating secrets immured in that calm and silent bosom. Slender and scarcely tall, she belonged to the order of spare, slight-made women, who hide within their slim frames an endowment of profound passion far exceeding that of their more voluptuously-formed sisters, who never coarsen into stoutness, and who at forty are as disturbing as at twenty. At this date Eva was twenty-six. She had a rather small, white face, which was a mask to the casual observer, and the very mirror of her feelings to anyone with eyes to read its signs.

'I tell you what you are like,' said Clive to her once: 'you are like a fine racehorse, always on the quiver.'

Yet many people considered her cold and impassive. Her walk and bearing showed a sensitive independence, and when she spoke it was usually in tones of command. The girls in the shop, where she was a power second only to Ezra Brunt, were a little afraid of her, chiefly because she poured terrible scorn on their small affectations, jealousies, and vendettas. But they liked her because, in their own phrase, 'there was no nonsense about' this redoubtable woman. She hated shams and make-believes with a bitter and ruthless hatred. She was the heiress to at least five thousand a year, and knew it well, but she never encouraged her father to complicate their simple mode of life with the pomps of wealth. They lived in a house with a large garden at Pireford, which is on the summit of the steep ridge between the Five Towns and Oldcastle, and they kept two servants and a coachman, who was also gardener. Eva paid the servants good wages, and took care to get good value therefore.

'It's not often I have any bother with my servants,' she would say, 'for they know that if there is any trouble I would just as soon clear them out and put on an apron and do the work myself.'

She was an accomplished house-mistress, and could bake her own bread: in towns not one woman in a thousand can bake. With the coachman she had little to do, for she could not rid herself of a sentimental objection to the carriage; it savoured of 'airs'; when she used it she used it as she might use a tramcar. It was her custom, every day except Saturday, to walk to the shop about eleven o'clock, after her house had been set in order. She had been thoroughly trained in the business, and had spent a year at a first-rate shop in High Street, Kensington. Millinery was her speciality, and she still watched over that department with a particular attention; but for some time past she had risen beyond the limitations of departments, and assisted her father in the general management of the vast concern. In commercial aptitude she resembled the typical Frenchwoman.

Although he was her father, Ezra Brunt had the wit to recognise her talents, and he always listened to her suggestions, which, however, sometimes startled him. One of them was that he should import into the Five Towns a modiste from Paris, offering a salary of two hundred a year. The old provincial stood aghast. He had the idea that all Parisian women were stage-dancers. And to pay four pounds a week to a female!

Nevertheless, Mademoiselle Bertot styled in the shop 'Madame' now presides over Ezra Brunt's dressmakers, draws her four pounds a week (of which she saves two), and by mere nationality has given a unique distinction and success to her branch of the business.

Eva occupied a small room opening off the principal showroom, and during hours of work she issued thence but seldom. Only customers of the highest importance might speak with her. She was a power felt rather than seen. Employes who knocked at her door always did so with a certain awe of what awaited them on the other side, and a consciousness that the moment was unsuitable for levity. 'If you please, Miss Eva'. Here she gave audience to the 'buyers' and window-dressers, listened to complaints and excuses, and occasionally had a secret orgy of afternoon tea with one or two of her friends. None but these few girls--mostly younger than herself, and remarkable only in that their dislike of the snobbery of the Five Towns, though less fiercely displayed, agreed with her own--really knew Eva. To them alone did she unveil herself, and by them she was idolized.

'She is simply splendid when you know her, such a jolly girl!' they would say to other people; but other people, especially other women, could not believe it. They fearfully respected her because she was very well dressed and had quantities of money. But they called her 'a curious creature'; it was inconceivable to them that she should choose to work in a shop; and her tongue had a causticity which was sometimes exceedingly disconcerting and mortifying. As for men, she was shy of them, and, moreover, she loathed the elaborate and insincere ritual of deference which the average man practises towards women unrelated to him, particularly when they are young and rich. Her father she adored, without knowing it; for he often angered her, and humiliated her in private. As for the rest, she was, after all, only six-and-twenty.

'If you don't mind, I should like to walk along with you,' Clive Timmis said to her one Sunday evening in the porch of the Bethesda Chapel.

'I shall be glad,' she answered at once; 'father isn't here, and I'm all alone.'

Ezra Brunt was indeed seldom there, counting in the matter of attendance at chapel among what were called 'the weaker brethren.'

'I am going over to Oldcastle,' Clive explained calmly.

So began the formal courtship more than a month after Clive had settled in Machin Street, for he was far too discreet to engender by precipitancy any suspicion in the haunts of scandal that his true reason for establishing himself in his uncle's household was a certain rich young woman who was to be found every day next door. Guided as much by instinct as by tact, Clive approached Eva with an almost savage simplicity and naturalness of manner, ignoring not only her father's wealth, but all the feigned punctilio of a wooer. His face said: 'Let there be no beating about the bush; I like you.' Hers answered: 'Good! we will see.'

From the first he pleased her, and not least in treating her exactly as she would have wished to be treated namely, as a quite plain person of that part of the middle class which is neither upper nor lower. Few men in the Five Towns would have been capable of forgetting Ezra Brunt's income in talking to Ezra Brunt's daughter. Fortunately, Timmis had a proud, confident spirit; the spirit of one who, unaided, has wrested success from the world's deathlike clutch. Had Eva the reversion of fifty thousand a year instead of five, he, Clive, was still a prosperous plain man, well able to support a wife in the position to which God had called him.

Their walks together grew more and more frequent, and they became intimate, exchanging ideas and rejoicing openly at the similarity of those ideas. Although there was no concealment in these encounters, still, there was a circumspection which resembled the clandestine. By a silent understanding Clive did not enter the house at Pireford; to have done so would have excited remark, for this house, unlike some, had never been the rendezvous of young men; much less, therefore, did he invade the shop. No! The chief part of their love-making (for such it was, though the term would have roused Eva's contemptuous anger) occurred in the streets; in this they did but follow the traditions of their class. Thus, the idyll, so matter-of-fact upon the surface, but within which glowed secret and adorable fires, progressed towards its culmination. Eva, the artless fool oh, how simple are the wisest at times! thought that the affair was hid from the shop. But was it possible? Was it possible that in those tiny bedrooms on the third floor, where the heavy evening hours were ever lightened with breathless interminable recitals of what some 'he' had said and some 'she' had replied, such an enthralling episode should escape discovery? The dormitories knew of Eva's 'attachment' before Eva herself. Yet none knew how it was known. The whisper arose like Venus from a sea of trivial gossip, miraculously, exquisitely. On the night when the first rumour of it traversed the passages there was scarcely any sleep at Brunt's, while Eva up at Pireford slumbered as a young girl.

On the Thursday afternoon with which we began, Brunt's was deserted save for the housekeeper and Eva, who was writing letters in her room.

'I saw you from my window, coming up the street,' she said to Clive, 'and so I ran down to open the door. Will you come into father's room? He is in Manchester for the day, buying.'

'I knew that,' said Timmis.

'How did you know?' She observed that his manner was somewhat nervous and constrained.

'You yourself told me last night don't you remember?'

'So I did.'

'That's why I sent the note round this morning to say I'd call this afternoon. You got it, I suppose?'

She nodded thoughtfully.

'Well, what is this business you want to talk about?'

It was spoken with a brave carelessness, but he caught the tremor in her voice, and saw her little hand shake as it lay on the table amid her father's papers. Without knowing why he should do so, he stepped hastily forward and seized that hand. Her emotion unmanned him. He thought he was going to cry; he could not account for himself.

'Eva,' he said thickly, 'you know what the business is; you know, don't you?'

She smiled. That smile, the softness of her hand, the sparkle in her eye, the heave of her small bosom. it was the divinest miracle! Clive, manufacturer of majolica, went hot and then cold, and then his wits were suddenly his own again.

'That's all right,' he murmured, and sighed, and placed on Eva's lips the first kiss that had ever lain there.

'Dear boy,' she said later, 'you should have come up to Pireford, not here, and when father was there.'

'Should I?' he answered happily. 'It just occurred to me all of a sudden this morning that you would be here, and that I couldn't wait.'

'You will come up to-night and see father?'

'I had meant to.'

'You had better go home now.'

'Had I?'

She nodded, putting her lips tightly together - a trick of hers.

'Come up about half-past eight.'

'Good! I will let myself out.'

He left her, and she gazed dreamily at the window, which looked on to a whitewashed yard. The next moment someone else entered the room with heavy footsteps. She turned round a little startled.

It was her father.

'Why! You are back early, father! How -' She stopped. Something in the old man's glance gave her a premonition of disaster. To this day she does not know what accident brought him from Manchester two hours sooner than usual, and to Machin Street instead of Pireford.

'Has young Timmis been here?' he inquired curtly.

'Yes.'

'Ha!' with subdued, sinister satisfaction, 'I saw him going out. He didna see me.' Ezra Brunt deposited his hat and sat down.

Intimate with all her father's various moods, she saw instantly and with terrible certainty that a series of chances had fatally combined themselves against her. If only she had not happened to tell Clive that her father would be at Manchester this day! If only her father had adhered to his customary hour of return! If only Clive had had the sense to make his proposal openly at Pireford some evening! If only he had left a little earlier! If only her father had not caught him going out by the side-door on a Thursday afternoon when the place was empty! Here, she guessed, was the suggestion of furtiveness which had raised her father's unreasoning anger, often fierce, and always incalculable.

'Clive Timmis has asked me to marry him, father.'

'Has he!'

'Surely you must have known, father, that he and I were seeing each other a great deal.'
'Not from your lips, my girl.'

'Well, father-' Again she stopped, this strong and capable woman, gifted with a fine brain to organize and a powerful will to command. She quailed, robbed of speech, before the causeless, vindictive, and infantile wrath of an old man who happened to be in a bad temper. She actually felt like a naughty schoolgirl before him. Such is the tremendous influence of lifelong habit, the irresistible power of the patria potestas when it has never been relaxed. Ezra Brunt saw in front of him only a cowering child. 'Clive is coming up to see you to-night,' she went on timidly, clearing her throat.

'Humph! Is he?'

The rosy and tender dream of five minutes ago lay in fragments at Eva's feet. She brooded with stricken apprehension upon the forms of obstruction which his despotism might choose.

The next morning Clive and his uncle breakfasted together as usual in the parlour behind, the chemist's shop.

'Uncle,' said Clive brusquely, when the meal was nearly finished, 'I'd better tell you that I've proposed to Eva Brunt.'

Old George Timmis lowered the Manchester Guardian and gazed at Clive over his steel-rimmed spectacles.

'She is a good girl,' he remarked; 'she will make you a good wife. Have you spoken to her father?'

'That's the point. I saw him last night, and I'll tell you what he said. These were his words: "You can marry my daughter, Mr. Timmis, when your uncle agrees to part with his shop!"'

'That I shall never do, nephew,' said the aged patriarch quietly and deliberately.

'Of course you won't, uncle. I shouldn't think of suggesting it. I'm merely telling you what he said.' Clive laughed harshly. 'Why,' he added, 'the man must be mad!'

'What did the young woman say to that?' his uncle inquired.

Clive frowned.

'I didn't see her last night,' he said. 'I didn't ask to see her. I was too angry.'

Just then the post arrived, and there was a letter for Clive, which he read and put carefully in his waistcoat pocket.

'Eva writes asking me to go to Pireford tonight,' he said, after a pause. 'I'll soon settle it, depend on that. If Ezra Brunt refuses his consent, so much the worse for him. I wonder whether he actually imagines that a grown man and a grown woman are to be.... Ah well, I can't talk about it! It's too silly. I'll be off to the works.'

When Clive reached Pireford that night, Eva herself opened the door to him. She was wearing a gray frock, and over it a large white apron, perfectly plain.

'My girls are both out to-night,' she said, 'and I was making some puffs for the sewing-meeting tea. Come into the breakfast-room.... This way,' she added, guiding him. He had entered the house on the previous night for the first time. She spoke hurriedly, and, instead of stopping in the breakfast-room, wandered uncertainly through it into the greenhouse, to which it gave access by means of a French window. In the dark, confined space, amid the close-packed blossoms, they stood together. She bent down to smell at a musk-plant. He took her hand and drew her soft and yielding form towards him and kissed her warm face.

'Oh, Clive!' she said. 'Whatever are we to do?'

'Do?' he replied, enchanted by her instinctive feminine surrender and reliance upon him, which seemed the more precious in that creature so proud and reserved to all others. 'Do! Where is your father?'

'Reading the _Signal_ in the dining-room.'

Every business man in the Five Towns reads the Staffordshire Signal from beginning to end every night.

'I will see him. Of course he is your father; but I will just tell him as decently as I can that neither you nor I will stand this nonsense.'

'You mustn't, you mustn't see him.'

'Why not?'

'It will only lead to unpleasantness.'

'That can't be helped.'

'He never, never changes when once he has said a thing. I know him.'

Clive was arrested by something in her tone, something new to him, that in its poignant finality seemed to have caught up and expressed in a single instant that bitterness of a lifetime's renunciation which falls to the lot of most women.

'Will you come outside?' he asked in a different voice.

Without replying, she led the way down the long garden, which ended in an ivy-grown brick wall and a panorama of the immense valley of industries below. It was a warm, cloudy evening. The last silver tinge of an August twilight lay on the shoulder of the hill to the left. There was no moon, but the splendid watch-fires of labour flamed from ore-heap and furnace across the whole expanse, performing their nightly miracle of beauty. Trains crept with noiseless mystery along the middle distance, under their canopies of yellow steam. Further off the far-extending streets of Hanbridge made a map of starry lines on the blackness. To the south-east stared the cold, blue electric lights of Knype railway-station. All was silent, save for a distant thunderous roar, the giant breathing of the forge at Cauldon Bar Ironworks.

Eva leaned both elbows on the wall and looked forth.

'Do you mean to say,' said Clive, 'that Mr. Brunt will actually stick by what he has said?'

'Like grim death,' said Eva.

'But what's his idea?'

'Oh! how can I tell you?' she burst out passionately.

'Perhaps I did wrong. Perhaps I ought to have warned him earlier, said to him, "Father, Clive Timmis is courting me!" Ugh! He cannot bear to be surprised about anything. But yet he must have known.... It was all an accident, Clive all an accident. He saw you leaving the shop yesterday. He would say he caught you leaving the shop, sneaking off like -'

'But, Eva'

'I know--I know! Don't tell me! But it was that, I am sure. He would resent the mere look of things, and then he would think and think, and the notion of your uncle's shop would occur to him again, after all these years. I can see his thoughts as plain. My dear, if he had not seen you at Machin Street yesterday, or if you had seen him and spoken to him, all might have gone right. He would have objected, but he would have given way in a day or two. Now he will never give way! I asked you just now what was to be done, but I knew all the time that there was nothing.'

'There is one thing to be done, Eva, and the sooner the better.'

'Do you mean that old Mr. Timmis must give up his shop to my father? Never! never!'

'I mean,' said Clive quietly, 'that we must marry without your father's consent.'

She shook her head slowly and sadly, relapsing into calmness.

'You shake your head, Eva, but it must be so.'

'I can't, my dear.'

'Do you mean to say that you will allow your father's childish whim for it's nothing else; he can't find any objection to me as a husband for you, and he knows it that you will allow his childish whim to spoil your life and mine? Remember, you are twenty-six and I am thirty-two.'

'I can't do it! I daren't! I'm mad with myself for feeling like this, but I daren't! And even if I dared I wouldn't. Clive, you don't know! You can't tell how it is!'

Her sorrowful, pathetic firmness daunted him. She was now composed, mistress again of herself, and her moral force dominated him.

'Then, you and I are to be unhappy all our lives, Eva?'

The soft influences of the night seemed to direct her voice as, after a long pause, she uttered the words: 'No one is ever quite unhappy in all this world.' There was another pause, as she gazed steadily down into the wonderful valley. 'We must wait.'

'Wait!' echoed Clive with angry grimness. 'He will live for twenty years!'

'No one is ever quite unhappy in all this world,' she repeated dreamily, as one might turn over a treasure in order to examine it.

Now for the epilogue to the feud. Two years passed, and it happened that there was to be a Revival at the Bethesda Chapel. One morning the superintendent minister and the revivalist called on Ezra Brunt at his shop. When informed of their presence, the great draper had an impulse of anger, for, like many stouter chapel-goers than himself, he would scarcely tolerate the intrusion of religion into commerce. However, the visit had an air of ceremony, and he could not decline to see these ambassadors of heaven in his private room. The revivalist, a cheery, shrewd man, whose powers of organization were obvious, and who seemed to put organization before everything else, pleased Ezra Brunt at once.

'We want a specially good congregation at the opening meeting to-night,' said the revivalist. 'Now, the basis of a good congregation must necessarily be the regular pillars of the church, and therefore we are making a few calls this morning to insure the presence of our chief men the men of influence and position. You will come, Mr. Brunt, and you will let it be known among your employes that they will please you by coming too?'

Ezra Brunt was by no means a regular pillar of the Bethesda, but he had a vague sensation of flattery, and he consented; indeed, there was no alternative.

The first hymn was being sung when he reached the chapel. To his surprise, he found the place crowded in every part. A man whom he did not know led him to a wooden form which had been put in the space between the front pews and the Communion-rail. He felt strange there, and uneasy, apprehensive.

The usual discreet somnolence of the chapel had been disturbed as by some indecorous but formidable awakener; the air was electric; anything might occur. Ezra was astounded by the mere volume of the singing; never had he heard such singing. At the end of the hymn the congregation sat down, hiding their faces in expectation. The revivalist stood erect and terrible in the pulpit, no longer a shrewd, cheery man of the world, but the very mouthpiece of the wrath and mercy of God. Ezra's self-importance dwindled before that gaze, till, from a renowned magnate of the Five Towns, he became an item in the multitude of suppliants. He profoundly wished he had never come.

'Remember the hymn,' said the revivalist, with austere emphasis:

'"My richest gain I count but loss,
And pour contempt on all my pride."'

The admirable histrionic art with which he intensified the consonants in the last line produced a tremendous effect. Not for nothing was this man cerebrated throughout Methodism as a saver of souls. When, after a pause, he raised his hand and ejaculated, 'Let us pray,' sobs could be heard throughout the chapel. The Revival had begun.

At the end of a quarter of an hour Ezra Brunt would have given fifty pounds to be outside, but he could not stir; he was magnetized. Soon the revivalist came down from the pulpit and stood within the Communion-rail, whence he addressed the nearmost part of the people in low, soothing tones of persuasion. Apparently he ignored Ezra Brunt, but the man was convicted of sin, and felt himself melting like an icicle in front of a fire.

He recalled the days of his youth, the piety of his father and mother, and the long traditions of a stern Dissenting family. He had backslidden, slackened in the use of the means of grace, run after the things of this world. It is true that none of his chiefest iniquities presented themselves to him; he was quite unconscious of them even then; but the lesser ones were more than sufficient to overwhelm him. Class-leaders were now reasoning with stricken sinners, and Ezra, who could not take his eyes off the revivalist, heard the footsteps of those who were going to the 'inquiry-room' for more private counsel. In vain he argued that he was about to be ridiculous; that the idea of him, Ezra Brunt, a professed Wesleyan for half a century, being publicly 'saved' at the age of fifty-seven was not to be entertained; that the town would talk; that his business might suffer if for any reason he should be morally bound to apply to it too strictly the principles of the New Testament. He was under the spell. The tears coursed down his long cheeks, and he forgot to care, but sat entranced by the revivalist's marvellous voice. Suddenly, with an awful sob, he bent and hid his face in his hands. The spectacle of the old, proud man helpless in the grasp of profound emotion was a sight to rend the heart-strings.

'Brother, be of good cheer,' said a tremulous and benign voice above him. 'The love of God compasseth all things. Only believe.'

He looked up and saw the venerable face and long white beard of George Christopher Timmis.

Ezra Brunt shrank away, embittered and ashamed.

'I cannot,' he murmured with difficulty.

'The love of God is all-powerful.'

'Will it make you part with that bit o' property, think you?' said Ezra Brunt, with a kind of despairing ferocity.

'Brother,' replied the aged servant of God, unmoved, 'if my shop is in truth a stumbling-block in this solemn hour, you shall have it.'

Ezra Brunt was staggered.

'I believe! I believe!' he cried.

'Praise God!' said the chemist, with majestic joy.

Three months afterwards Eva Brunt and Clive Timmis were married. It is characteristic of the fine sentimentality which underlies the surface harshness of the inhabitants of the Five Towns that, though No. 54 Machin Street was duly transferred to Ezra Brunt, the chemist retiring from business, he has never rebuilt it to accord with the rest of his premises. In all its shabbiness it stands between the other big dazzling shops as a reminding monument.

Printed in Great Britain
by Amazon